JONNY JAKES

THE OLD SCHOOL GHOUL

Published in the United States in 2016 by Stone Arch Books,
A Capstone Imprint
1710 Roe Crest Drive
North Mankato, Minnesota 56003
www.mycapstone.com

First published in 2015 by Curious Fox,
an imprint of Capstone Global Library Limited
264 Banbury Road, Oxford, OX2 7DY
Registered company number 6695582
www.curious-fox.com

Text © 2016 Malcolm Judge
Illustrations © 2016 Capstone

Library of Congress Cataloging-in-Publication Data is available on
the Library of Congress website.

ISBN: 978-1-4965-2829-2 (library binding)
ISBN: 978-1-4965-2830-8 (paperback)
ISBN: 978-1-4965-2831-5 (eBook PDF)

Illustrated by Alan Brown - Advocate Art
Designed by Tracy McCabe

Printed in the United States of America in North Mankato, Minnesota.
009659F16

JONNY JAKES

Investigates

THE OLD SCHOOL GHOUL

Malcolm Judge

STONE ARCH BOOKS
a capstone imprint

To Dom

Tuesday, January 8th

National Bubble Bath Day
I'll accidentally mention it really loudly outside
the geography office.

I'm Jonny Jakes.

If you think I'm telling you my real name, think again.

I'm an undercover reporter for *The Woodford Word*. It's
the unofficial newspaper for Woodford School.

Last semester I
saved the world
from being eaten
by a family of
bloodthirsty aliens.
Today I got a bunch
of homework and
had mystery meat
casserole for
lunch.

Apparently life
isn't fair.

On the plus side, we sold a lot of newspapers. Julie Singh figures we sold over one hundred thousand copies.

That's a lot of quarters.

We had a meeting at the end of last semester to decide what to do with the money. I said that as Editor and Chief Executive of *The Woodford Word*, I should get most of the money so I can invest it in the paper's future. Julie thought it was only fair to share the money equally between all of us.

She's like that.

Sally Coyle got out her calculator and pushed a few buttons. She said that, using a formula that accounted for how long each of us had worked on the paper, as well as factoring in the seniority of my position, her calculations suggested I was eligible to receive 56.34 percent of the profit margin.

Norris told her to speak English.

I asked Sally if we were talking about a jar full of cash or a bucketful.

She said I'd probably have enough money to fill up a medium-sized suitcase.

I agreed that it seemed like a very good formula.

As soon as I got home with the money, I went to work on a new disguise. I needed to look like a flashy businessman. I had the false mustache, I had the mirrored sunglasses, and I had a slightly smaller version of my dad's old wedding suit that mysteriously went missing from his closet last summer.

Most importantly, I had a suitcase full of cash.

I wheeled the suitcase into town, doing my best to act cool. It's not easy when you're pulling half a ton of quarters behind you. Once I'd got my breath back,

I went into the gigantic computer store and snapped my fingers at the nearest employee. He didn't look very pleased about it, but I had a character to keep up.

I asked him for three new laptops, a top-of-the-line telescopic camera, and an industrial-sized photocopier. I wanted them brought over when I knew my parents would be out visiting my grandma. I took off my shades, gave him a wink, and told him I'd make it worth his while if he could get them all delivered to my house in a white, unmarked van at 2:30 p.m. on Sunday, no questions asked.

He said he was going to call the police.

Then I opened my suitcase.

I could get used to being rich.

It's not easy being famous and trying to keep your true identity a secret. Thanks to *The Woodford Word*, everyone knows that I saved the world by defeating Mr. Jones and his evil horde of flesh-eating children.

THE WOODFORD WORD

JONNY JAKES SAVES THE WORLD

Not content with defending truth and justice, undercover schoolboy reporter Jonny Jakes has now saved the world.

But no one has the faintest idea what I look like because they were all in a weird hamburger-induced daze at the time. All kinds of shady people are offering a reward for any information that might lead to the discovery of my real name.

Luckily, no one thinks an eleven-year-old is capable of award-winning journalism.

Norris can't understand why I don't just come forward and get all the glory. He says I could get myself on one of those TV shows where celebrities goof off and make fools of themselves in front of millions of viewers.

I told him it was embarrassing enough walking through the middle of Woodford every day wearing a school uniform that's exactly the same color as barf.

Maybe I'll think about it when my skin stops erupting with zits at the sight of french fries. Or when I feel the need to impress girls.

Mom keeps reminding me that's about to happen any day now.

Speaking of girls, there's one in particular I'm trying to avoid. Michelle Bell.

Every time I see her, I have to dive for cover. She doesn't know I'm Jonny Jakes, but she does know I have something to do with *The Woodford Word*. She found me and Norris intercepting letters from our old principal, Mr. Hardy, last semester and threatened to tell if she didn't get her own fashion spread in the paper. I'm hoping because *The Woodford Word* helped save her from aliens, she'll keep her mouth shut.

Unfortunately that doesn't happen very often.

Unbelievable! Karl Huck is going to pretend to be me. Julie heard it in the lunch line.

Karl Huck has more stupid ideas than actual brain cells to have them with. In December, he swapped the star on top of the school holiday tree with a pair of his underwear. He thought it would be funny. Everyone else just wished he'd remembered to wash them first.

Being Karl Huck, he hadn't realized that his mom had sewn a name tag into them. He got suspended for a week.

It made a great front page for the festive issue of *The Woodford Word*, though:

THE WOODFORD WORD

UNLUCKY HUCKY

Karl Huck decided to add his own decoration to the school's holiday tree this week: his tighty-whities. Unluckily for him, his mom wasn't too excited about him just leaving them lying around.

I guess he wants payback.

Norris volunteered to get a hold of Karl's flash drive. If he's put any fake *Woodford Word* material on it, we can use it to expose him. Julie said she'd mention Karl's name at home to see if it got any reaction from her mom. Julie's mom, Mrs. Singh, is the principal's secretary and talks loudly about everything.

That's the main reason I let Julie work for the paper.

Sally said she'd ask her friends to see if she could find out anything useful. I said I didn't think she had any friends. She said she knows Andrea Mollov from swimming, who is best friends with Molly Shearer, who used to walk into school with someone who lived across the road from Karl Huck.

I won't hold my breath.

If I can get enough material together for a paper, at least the headline won't be difficult:

HUCK SUCKS

Time to get to work.

Thursday, January 10th

Another year and already another triumph for *The Woodford Word*. We managed to get the paper out this morning, and Karl Huck is now officially the least popular guy in school.

Or he would be, if he wasn't at home pretending to be sick.

Just because Norris Morris is really big, has a silly name, and smiles a lot, everyone thinks he's stupid. People underestimate him. That's how Norris managed to get Karl Huck out of the computer room yesterday. He told Huck that he'd been ordered to go over to Mr. Hamed's office to pick up a long weight.

Huck would still be waiting there now if the custodian hadn't explained.

Norris found Karl's so-called "newspaper" on the flash drive he'd left behind. Karl had used all his brainpower to encrypt it in a file named "DROWDROFDOOWEHT."

Karl Huck wouldn't know what cunning was if it jumped out in front of him in bright yellow boxing gloves and broke his nose.

According to him, good headlines to use would've been:

WE'RE TIE-RED OF TIES

for an article complaining about having to wear uniforms;

MISSING MUNCHIES

for a story complaining about how the vending machine keeps breaking; and

PICS AND KICKS

about how the JV football team had their picture in the local paper before the second game of the County Cup tournament.

I've never been so insulted in my life.

As well as exposing Karl's plan to trick everyone, we blew up a picture Sally had found of him when he was a toddler. It's perfect. He's sitting at a table, trying to do some drawing with a really big pen. But there's nothing on the paper in front of him, and he's looking really frustrated.

That's because he's holding the pen upside-down.

THE WOODFORD WORD

HUCK SUCKS!

In a clumsy attempt to impersonate *The Woodford Word's* star reporter, Karl Huck has once again come off second best.

I think Sally's starting to get the hang of the newspaper business.

Friday, January 11th

I still have one resolution left.
That's a new record.

Michelle Bell was lying in wait for me today.

She was hiding behind the penguin sculpture as I came out of the library after my study period. Just because I've got something to do with a newspaper, she thinks I'm a nerd.

"I want a word with you, nerd!" she sneered, grabbing my tie and pinning me against the wall.

"Go for it," I wheezed, trying to sound casual despite the lack of oxygen reaching my brain.

"You've been avoiding me," she hissed, covering me in spit.

"Sorry. It's just my mom told me to keep away from people who try to strangle me."

"And I will if you don't shut up and listen," she spat again, giving me an extra shove against the wall.

I decided to shut up and listen.

"That paper you work for hasn't been very nice about my boyfriend!"

"But . . . we . . ." I attempted to protest. "We haven't written anything about Trevor Neave."

"My *new* boyfriend," Michelle clarified. "And I don't like it when people are mean to my boyfriends. So, you tell them that I want to know who Jonny Jakes is, or I'm going to see what happens when I pull this even tighter."

She pulled the knot on my tie hard up against my neck and then suddenly released me. She marched off as I crumpled against the penguin and scratched my face on one of the flippers.

I hate that stupid penguin.

I told Norris how we were going to deal with the Michelle Bell situation.

He said he didn't hit girls.

He said he knew Michelle Bell was going out with Karl Huck. I asked him why. He said it paid to keep up with other people's love lives, because you never knew when that kind of information might come in handy.

I don't know how Michelle Bell keeps up with her own love life.

I called an emergency board meeting at the picnic table next to the wildlife garden. One day *The Woodford Word* will get the office space it truly deserves.

"So, what are we going to do about her?" I asked. "If she opens her mouth, it's going to be a disaster."

"We'd still keep the paper going without you," Sally piped up enthusiastically.

"You see what I mean!" I yelled, banging my fist on the table.

"Hey! We're quite capable of doing things without you, thank you very much," Julie complained.

"Oh, sure you are! Just like you came up with something on Karl Huck when it really mattered."

Julie went a little red in the face. "Actually, I did have something, but . . ."

"But what?" I demanded. "He was about to ruin our reputation!"

"But I wasn't sure you'd handle it in a sensitive manner," Julie said quietly. "In fact, I'm not sure you're capable of handling anything in a sensitive manner."

Julie had gone beet red in the face. I thought about shouting "BEEEET FAAAACE!" but I had a feeling it might've proved her point.

Julie took a deep breath and continued.

"It's just, I'm not sure I want to be part of a newspaper that's always pointing out all the bad things about the school. I mean, would it kill us just to be positive for a change?"

I couldn't believe what I was hearing.

"What about our coverage on the boy's field hockey team winning the regional championship against the Southton Fire?" I pointed out. "That was definitely a positive story."

"That wasn't positive," Julie moaned. "The headline was 'How Dire Is Fire?'"

"The Southton players couldn't even hold their sticks the right way — a few were holding them upside-down!"

"That's not the point!"

"Yes it is!" I insisted. "We only beat them because their own defender forgot which way he was supposed to hit the puck and scored on his own goal!" I was getting pretty red in the face myself now. "There is such a thing as the truth, you know, or can't you handle it? And the truth is, we only won that game because the other team was even worse than we were!"

Me and Julie were face to face now and breathing heavily. You could have cut the air with a breadstick.

Sally coughed. "Actually, it's a ball."

"What?!" me and Julie shouted, still glaring at each other.

"It's only called a puck in ice hockey," Sally whispered.

If Sally had been trying to clear the air, it hadn't worked. Julie gave me one last glare, then turned on her heel and left. Sally hesitated and then ran after her.

I asked Norris if he was absolutely sure he didn't hit girls.

Sunday, January 13th

I've spent the weekend wondering how to deal with Michelle Bell. If she starts using my name in connection with *The Woodford Word*, my Jonny Jakes days are over.

I needed to cheer myself up, so I Googled myself again and surfed through the millions of articles and pictures about my famous victory over Mr. Jones. You could actually see me in some of them, but without a big arrow pointing it out, no one would ever know who I really was.

And all it took to change that was Michelle Bell and her big mouth.

I decided to check the pictures for ones of her. To throw darts at them.

That's when I found it. I was looking through an online Japanese newspaper site. The Japanese love me. There was a picture of a busy school hallway. It was the day the school reopened. Everyone's still looking kind of shell-shocked. And there, standing near the bottom of the stairs, was Michelle Bell.

It wasn't just the dumb look on her face. It wasn't all the extra pudginess after being fed a diet of mega-fattening hamburgers. Everyone still had that. It was the fact she'd forgotten to straighten her hair.

And when Michelle Bell forgets to straighten her hair, she looks like an electrocuted poodle.

Monday, January 14th

This time, it was my turn to lie in wait for Michelle Bell. I hid behind the recycling bins at recess and waited for her to reapply her makeup. It didn't take long.

"Remember me?" I said, reaching into my pocket and holding up a copy of her picture between my fingers. "You know, the guy you tried to strangle behind the penguin?"

Michelle Bell looked confused, so I pressed home my advantage.

"It's not very nice being threatened, is it?"

I'd hoped for some kind of reaction, but Michelle Bell didn't seem to be bothered. She pulled an eyeliner pencil out of her makeup bag and pointed it at my raised hand.

"Why are you waving a candy wrapper at me, you moron?"

I cursed my stupidity and reached back in my pocket for the picture.

"What's that supposed to be?" Michelle demanded when I finally managed to pull out the crumpled photo.

"It's a picture. Of you."

"So what?" Michelle grunted, unimpressed.

"Take a closer look," I said, and tossed the picture toward her.

It would've been cooler if it hadn't fallen right into a puddle.

I picked the picture out of the puddle, wiped it, and passed it over. Michelle Bell brought it slowly to her face. Her eyes widened, and she let out a tiny gasp.

At last I had her at my mercy.

Her fingers were up my nostrils so quickly, I didn't even have time to blink. Michelle Bell put the picture right in front of my watering eyes.

"If anyone else sees this, I'll rip your nose clean off your face."

I tried to say, "If you kill me, we will publish this picture every day for a month," but I think it just sounded like, "AAAAAAAAAAAAAAAAAHHHHHHH!"

"What?"

It was pointless trying to talk with silver glitter fingers up my nose. It was hard enough trying to breathe. I pulled out the piece of paper Norris made me carry in my pocket. He'd warned me that this kind of thing might happen.

"'If I get hurt, we will publish this picture every day for a month,'" Michelle Bell read. She thought about it, then reluctantly let me go.

"You know, one day I'm going to find out who that Jonny Jakes is. And when I do, I'm gonna . . ."

She didn't finish her sentence. Imagination isn't Michelle Bell's strong point.

"Get lost!" she snarled, ripping up the picture and tossing it in the nearest trash can.

It wasn't going to be easy in the school playground, but I gave it a try.

After lunch, we had an assembly. We used to have them in the morning occasionally, but now it's part of Mr. Chattersly's new routine, along with compulsory water bottles and letting the twelfth graders call him Alistair.

Mr. Chattersly is the acting principal.

That means he isn't our actual principal, but it hasn't stopped him from changing everything.

"Now then, everybody," Mr. Chattersly began. "Let's just pause to reflect for a moment, shall we?"

Mr. Chattersly paused for reflection and swept back his wavy brown hair with one hand. I'm pretty sure the main reason Mr. Chattersly pauses to reflect is just so that he can sweep back his wavy brown hair with one hand.

"It strikes me," Mr. Chattersly continued, "that we live in a time that values cynicism over positivity. A time that encourages putting something down, rather than building something up. A time, you could say, that prefers sneering over cheering."

Mr. Chattersly thinks he has a way with words. That's why he uses so many of them.

"But I want to change all that. You all know I'm a history teacher, so you won't be surprised that I think we can learn a great deal from studying the past.

"When Woodford School was founded in 1848, this country was very proud of itself, and for good reason! It was a time of discovery and innovation, and the possibilities for our infant nation seemed endless. Ask anyone back then what he thought of his country, and he'd tell you it was the home of all that was great and good, rich with freedom and opportunity for all.

"So, I was thinking, why don't we try to be like those prideful, hopeful Americans? I don't mean let's all grow bushy sideburns and wear top hats." Mr. Chattersly left a brief pause so that everyone could laugh.

When nobody did, he turned it into a longer pause and tried to make it look like that's what he meant to do in the first place. Then he added some pacing up and down and wagging a finger at nothing in particular.

"I mean, of course," he said, struggling to get back into his rhythm, "let's try to *think* a little more like those early Americans, shall we? Rather than think the worst of ourselves, why don't we try celebrating our good side? Let's not be afraid of singing our own praises! Let's not be afraid of banging our own drum! And, most of all, let's not be afraid of blowing our own trumpet."

Mr. Chattersly thumped his fist on the podium. He was pumped up again.

"And so, to encourage a new spirit of optimism and school pride, I am hereby launching a competition to create a new, official school newspaper. Yes! You heard me!" Mr. Chattersly cried triumphantly as his audience slowly came back to life, and Matthew Roberts stopped trying to flick my ears.

"We thank Jonny Jakes for what he did last semester, but no more can the only voice among us be one of smart comments and put-downs. We need a newspaper to take us forward, not hold us back. A newspaper to raise us up, not knock us down.

"Therefore, I am proposing to offer the position of Editor, as well as access to a not insubstantial amount of money from a special school fund, to whoever can put the best newspaper on my desk by the end of school on Thursday!"

When Mr. Chattersly had finished, there was a lot of excited murmuring. His big idea had gone down well. I got away before there was any chance I might bump into Julie Singh.

It wasn't as if I actually needed to see the smug look on her face.

 Tuesday, January 15th

Mr. Chattersly's going to have a lot of newspapers to choose from.

And they're all going to be completely crappy choices.

I thought Karl Huck's headlines were bad, but they're masterpieces compared to some of the ones I've heard today. Who knew that "Tuesday" could be spelled in so many stupid ways?

The only person who worries me is Hari Patel. He can actually write a little bit, and he's usually more than happy to let everyone know about it. Norris says he isn't doing anything yet.

That's what worries me.

Norris asked me why I wasn't taking part in the competition.

I had to give him a lecture about the importance of intellectual integrity, freedom of speech, and not wanting to write establishment propaganda, but I don't think he was really listening.

He just said I was chicken.

Wednesday, January 16th

Ivan the Terrible named Tsar of Russia, 1547
Back when people had real names.

Hari Patel is definitely up to something.

I was keeping a close eye on him in English. He was
acting strange. He had this far-away look in his eyes,
and every now and again you could see his lips twitch.
It was almost like he didn't care about how Shirley
Jackson was using symbolism in "The Lottery."

I tried to find him at lunch, but there was no sign of
him anywhere. Not even with the Creative Writing Club.
It was the same during every passing period.

I gave up and suggested to Norris that we follow Julie
instead. I hadn't seen her around for a while, either.
Normally I can't seem to get away from her, but it was
like she'd vanished.

I told him it would be just like her to take advantage
of all the help I'd given her at *The Woodford Word*
and use it to stab me in the back by trying to start her

own newspaper. Even worse, it would probably be one of those papers telling everyone how amazing and wonderful they all were.

Norris said that maybe Mr. Chattersly's competition was just making me a little paranoid and that I shouldn't forget who my friends are.

I told him that he was desperate for me to fail, just like everyone else, and stormed off.

I think I proved my point.

Thursday, January 17th

When I got to school, Julie was waiting for me by the front doors with Norris and Sally. I figured her conscience must've finally caught up with her, so I waited for the apology.

"Hi," she said, and then stopped.

I waited.

"Oh, come on, you guys. Work it out!" Sally pleaded. "Say you're sorry, and let's get on with the paper."

"Just swallow your pride and get it over with," Norris muttered to me.

"Get what over with?" I asked.

"The apology," he said.

"Hey, I'm ready whenever she is," I complained. "Why don't you tell *her* to hurry it up?"

Julie turned to look at Norris and Sally.

That's when I realized they all thought *I* was the one who should be saying sorry. I couldn't believe it.

"What do I need to be sorry for?" I shouted. "She's the one who keeps criticizing me."

"I just wanted you to be a bit more constructive," Julie said. "You didn't have to bite my head off."

"I didn't bite your head off. I just pointed out that I happen to believe in telling the truth."

"You were rude, you shouted in my face, and you said I couldn't handle the truth."

"Well, can you?" I asked.

"Well, can *you*?" she asked back.

We were face to face again. Norris and Sally tried to step in between us.

"Can you handle the truth that you're just a stuck-up little nobody who thinks he's better than everyone else?" Julie snarled, stomping on Norris's foot and pushing him out of the way.

"Sure I can!" I yelled back, giving Sally a jab with my elbow. "Just as long as *you* can handle the truth that you're an interfering know-it-all!"

I'd have been happy to go on discussing the issue, but we were starting to draw a crowd. I decided to settle the whole matter there and then.

"Listen, as far as I'm concerned, I have a paper to run, and you're either with me or against me. If you're with me, let's go and find out what Hari's up to. If you're not, then leave me alone and let me get on with my job."

There was an uncomfortable silence.

Then everyone left me alone and let me get on with my job.

I needed a place to think, so I dropped in to the Drop-In Zone. It's a room with lots of brightly colored cushions where you can talk to a teacher about anything that's bothering you.

The place was deserted.

I sat on the star-shaped cushion and tried to get Julie

Singh out of my head. It wasn't easy. The cushions would have been perfect for throwing at her dumb, interfering face.

I could even hear her voice. It was nagging me. Asking me why I was so bothered by Hari. Telling me I was jealous because he'd won a short story competition and that I felt threatened by the fact that he likes to read Shakespeare for fun.

I tried to focus. I came to the conclusion that there was no point in trying to follow Hari anymore. There was only one day left, so he'd probably finished his paper already. That's when I realized I didn't need to find Hari.

I just needed to find his paper.

And a pretty good place to look was probably going to be the big red box marked NEWSPAPER COMPETITION on the table outside Mr. Chattersly's office.

A group of tenth graders were hanging around the hall when I arrived, so I pretended to look at some internet safety posters. When they left, I made my way over to the red box.

It was full of manila envelopes. I quickly flicked through the top three.

The first two were pretty similar. Cindy Loi had *Well HELLO Woodford*, and Kerys Gosforth's effort was called *Way To Go, Woodford*. They both involved people smiling way too much.

The third one was from Steven Frost. He hadn't quite mastered the idea of a catchy title, but at least he was letting his readers know exactly what they were going to get with *Steven Frost's Focus on Sports and Music at Woodford School*.

Then I found what I was looking for.

I checked around to see if I was by myself. The coast was clear, but I still made a big show of putting my empty envelope into the box while at the same time sneaking Hari's envelope out. Then I headed for the Drop-In Zone.

I opened Hari's envelope carefully so I could tape it back up and replace it when I was done. It felt good to be back in control again. I pulled the paper out.

I don't know what I was expecting, but it wasn't what was in front of me. I flipped through a few pages just to see if they were an improvement on the first, but if anything, they were worse. The whole thing was based around a dog named Nifty the News Hound that Hari had tried to make look cool.

He'd tried way too hard.

Nifty had sunglasses, a baseball cap, and pants so low you could see the top of his butt crack.

His hairy butt crack.

If that wasn't bad enough, the name of the paper and every article was written like a speech bubble coming out of Nifty's mouth. There was even a picture of him at the bottom of each page with the slogan "*I've got a nose for news!*"

I flicked to the back pages where Nifty had a sports round-up. At the end of each item, there was a WOOF rating from one to five for sporting achievement. Everyone scored a five. Even Patrick Raymond, who'd apparently "battled through difficult circumstances" to lose his badminton match three games to nil.

On closer inspection, the "difficult circumstances" were

that his opponent could play badminton.

I let out a sigh of relief. I admit it; I'd been scared I was going to have some actual competition.

What I'm not scared of is a stupid talking dog.

Friday, January 18th

For once, the school couldn't wait for Mr. Chattersly's assembly. Everyone was talking about who was going to win. After lunch, I got to the auditorium early. I wanted to watch all the gory details.

That sure backfired.

Mr. Chattersly was early too. He was pacing up and down more than normal. There was a large projector screen pulled down behind him, and he tapped a remote control on the palm of his hand.

He looked happy. Too happy.

As everyone else filed in, I looked out for Hari Patel. I wanted to watch his reaction, but I couldn't spot him. I could see Julie and Sally sitting nearby, but they were both determined not to see me.

When the noise had settled down a little, Mr. Chattersly paused and reflected for a moment. Everyone else waited for him to get on with it.

When he was done, Mr. Chattersly did a dramatic hair sweep and looked out eagerly over the students in front of him.

Too eagerly.

"I'm delighted to see that you're all as excited as I am about our new school newspaper," he began confidently. "I'm pleased to tell you that the winning entry is very exciting indeed. But before I reveal who's won, I'd like to thank all of you who decided to enter. I had a most enjoyable time reading over all your efforts. Well done!"

The people who'd entered the competition were surrounded by their friends. Cindy Loi's clique were giving each other small little claps, and Kerys Gosforth was in the middle of a group hug. Steven Frost's buddies were punching him on the arm as hard as they could.

"But there has to be a winner," Mr. Chattersly continued, "and that winner is . . ."

Mr. Chattersly did a big pause like they do on cheesy reality TV shows and pretended he didn't know who the winner of his own competition was. I bet half the school was expecting glitter cannons to go off.

He stretched the silence to the breaking point.

Then all of a sudden, it was over.

"Hari Patel!"

Hari jumped out from behind the curtains at the back of the stage. Despite the lack of glitter, Hari was still eager to play up his big moment. He raised his arms out wide and joined in with the whooping.

Actually, I'm pretty sure he did most of it himself.

Once he'd managed to shut Hari up, Mr. Chattersly attempted to calm the school down.

"Okay, okay. Well done, Hari," he said, patting at the air with his hands. "Now then, let's take a look at what Hari's come up with."

Mr. Chattersly pointed the remote control at the projector. I turned my head the other way and got ready to drink in the disappointment on everyone's faces.

That's probably why it took me a while to realize that Nifty the News Hound wasn't there.

Instead, there was a picture of a student. One side of him was dressed in the Woodford School uniform: vomit-green blazer, white button-up shirt, tie, and black pants. The other side of him was dressed in old-fashioned brown dress shoes, long gray socks, gray knickers, a white collarless shirt, a gray jacket, and a brown cap.

Above the boy was the headline:

WOODFORD NOW AND WHEN

Mr. Chattersly gazed out over the eight hundred and forty-six faces who were trying to decide if their new school newspaper was brilliant or bonkers. While Mr. Chattersly took in the view, Hari picked up the microphone.

"The idea is," he shouted, "that we report what's happening in the school *now*, as well as what happened back when the school first started. If you turn to page three, for instance, there's an article about how many students the school started with compared to how many students there are today."

Mr. Chattersly came over to Hari and took the microphone back.

"And the great thing about Hari's idea is that he wants *you* to help him with the research. We know a few things about how Woodford School began but, with *Woodford*

Now and When, we can all work together and learn a whole lot more. It's inspired!"

As Mr. Chattersly went for his hair, Hari grabbed the microphone back.

"I did have another idea: some garbage about a stupid dog called Nifty the News Hound. I'd just like to apologize to anyone if they got the wrong idea about that." Hari's eyes sparkled maliciously as he finally gave up the microphone to Mr. Chattersly.

Mr. Chattersly swept his hair back and did his best sincere face.

"Yes, we were a little worried that Jonny Jakes might try to spoil things, so I'm afraid we put a few decoys in the competition box as well as the real ones. However," Mr. Chattersly continued, "I'm happy to see that Mr. Jakes has decided not to ruin things today and has been gracious in his absence."

That was the final straw. No one calls me gracious and gets away with it.

Sunday, January 20th

James Cook discovers the Hawaii Islands, 1778
Then he stupidly called them the Sandwich Islands.

It's been a bad weekend.

Yesterday I invited Norris over for a working dinner. He said he needed time to consider whether he wanted to work with me again. I said Dad was going to make pancakes.

"So, what do you think?" I asked Norris when I'd finally gotten him away from the maple syrup.

"Amazing!" he said, shutting his eyes and licking his lips. "Fluffy and yet somehow gooey at the same time."

"Not the pancakes — the paper!" I yelled, slapping a copy of *Woodford Now and When* on the bed in front of him.

"Oh, pretty good, I guess," he mumbled, picking at his teeth with his fingernail. "I haven't read it yet."

"How is it pretty good if you haven't read it?" I wanted to know.

"Well, it's a clever idea. Woodford School now and Woodford School then. Clever."

"But what are we going to do about it?"

Norris didn't seem to understand the question.

"Nothing."

"What do you mean, nothing?" I said, trying to keep my voice down. "We can't just sit here and do *nothing*."

Norris picked up Hari's paper and flicked through a few pages. Then he lowered it back down.

"We're not going to do anything about it because there's nothing wrong with it. *The Woodford Word* has a rival. So what? *You'll* just have to try to make it better."

"Better? What do you mean?" I protested. "*The Woodford Word* is the best newspaper at Woodford School. Always has been. Always will be."

"Then there's nothing to be scared of, is there?" Norris said casually, scraping a stray blob of syrup off his jeans and sticking it back in his mouth.

"I'm not scared of *him*, if that's what you think," I said, ripping Hari's picture off the back page and thrusting it at Norris.

"Right," Norris said, smiling even more than usual. "Sure you're not."

That's the last time I invite him over for pancakes.

As if Saturday hadn't been bad enough, this morning Dad taught me how to mow the lawn. It's going to be my new chore.

I've spent the rest of the day mourning the loss of my childhood.

Monday, January 21st
Martin Luther King Day

Taking time to honor a true champion of justice.

Tuesday, January 22nd

I woke up determined not to think about *Woodford Now and When*. I decided to count things instead. I now know that, on average, Mom sighs three times a minute, I chew my breakfast three hundred and twelve times, and there are five hundred and fifty-six white tiles in the bathroom.

Dad decided to use the downstairs toilet in the end.

I was doing okay at school right up until Stephanie Roland burst into homeroom. She had the latest edition of *Woodford Now and When* with her. On the front, were pictures of two men. One was Mr. Chattersly, and the other one was this really stern-looking guy named Victory Piggot. Apparently he was the school's first principal.

SCHOOLYARD SHOWDOWN!

On pages two and three, Hari put the principals up against each other in a mock contest. Mr. Chattersly scored points for not thrashing his students with a stick, but Victory Piggot came out on top because he had a cooler name and enough facial hair to house a family of squirrels.

Everyone thought it was awesome and barged in to get a closer look. In fact, there were so many people crowded around, it's a miracle no one was injured when I somehow managed to trip over the table leg and completely shred the paper with the compass I was stupidly waving around in my outstretched hand.

By lunchtime, there wasn't anyone without a copy of *Woodford Now and When*. I'd had to get one myself so that I didn't stand out. Norris said that's why he had one too, but I think he was just trying to make me feel better.

There were details about how every week "one lucky reader" would be featured in the "Special Guest" column if they could come up with a good enough article and were prepared to use their real name.

That means two depressing things:

1. Now everyone's going to think they can be a journalist.
2. (And even worse) everyone's going to keep on buying Hari's paper to see if they're in it.

Wednesday, January 23rd

If Hari Patel gets any more big-headed, they're going to have to widen the halls.

By about a mile.

Thursday, January 24th

And if he comes into *one* more class whooping and high-fiving whoever can't get out of his way fast enough, then I simply won't be responsible for my actions.

Friday, January 25th

Henry VIII marries Anne Boleyn, 1533
Three years later he cuts off her head.

The latest edition of *Woodford Now and When* came out this morning.

I could hardly contain my excitement.

"Look at this!" Norris said, waving his copy at me.

"Make me."

"Read it," Norris insisted.

"I don't want to read it. I want it to go away."

"Trust me. You'll want to read this."

Norris had Hari's paper open to the first special guest reporter's article on page five. It didn't look like he was going to give up, so I took the paper.

"It has a horrible title," I said.

"I know. Keep reading," Norris replied.

According to the article, Victory Piggot had not only been in the *Rotherby and Woodford Herald* almost every week, but he'd made the national newspapers several times with reports on his students' academic achievements and his "outspoken" remarks on "the importance of applying radical modern scientific discoveries to the educational establishments of this great country."

Victory Piggot's Claims to Fame

Former principal Victory Piggot was something of a minor celebrity. According to our research,

There were a couple of grainy old pictures of Piggot from the papers. He was puffing his chest out and trying to look really unhappy.

"Keep going," Norris instructed.

I read the last three paragraphs. They were annoyingly interesting.

The last time Victory Piggot was big news was in 1872. This time it had nothing to do with his views on education or the outstanding performance of his students.

It had a lot to do with him disappearing off the face of the earth.

The article said that, "despite several investigations," his disappearance was a total mystery. No body was ever found and no foul play was ever suspected. One newspaper had commented:

The only suspicious circumstance in the disappearance of respected principal Victory Piggot is that there are no suspicious circumstances. In previous cases where a prominent individual has disappeared, investigations have usually uncovered probable cause for the disappearance, even if they have not discovered the person themselves.

"Okay, I finished," I said to Norris, who seemed to be waiting for something.

"No you haven't."

"How do you know?"

"Because you haven't shouted anything yet."

"Why am I going to shout?" I wanted to know.

"Look at the bottom of the page."

I looked at the bottom of the page. I shouted. I shouted something very rude.

You know how sometimes your life is going well and then a girl comes along and ruins it? I thought so.

Julie Singh is Hari Patel's first special guest columnist.

And now, thanks to her story of his mysterious disappearance, Victory Piggot fever is taking over the school. Everyone has their own theory about what must have happened to him. Mrs. McKeane was so excited, she forced the whole class to write a story about it.

Mine finished with a slow and painful death.

The latest craze is to do an impression of him. It mostly involves crossing your arms, staring like you're in a bad mood, and then trying to cane somebody with your pencil case before running away and mysteriously disappearing.

I'm glad it's Friday. My butt can't take much more.

Saturday, January 26th

I asked Norris to come over for a sleepover. Mom said she was glad to see me having fun with my friends for once.

I didn't tell her it was a research-based sleepover.

"So, what exactly are we researching?" Norris asked as he booted up his laptop and ripped open three gigantic bags of candy.

"Victory Piggot's dirty secrets. What do you think?"

"But what if he was just a really good principal?" Norris complained.

"If he was so wonderful, why did he disappear?" I pointed out. "People disappear when somebody has something against them or when they're in some kind of trouble."

Norris grunted something back, but it got lost in a fistful of gummy bears.

By midnight, the only dirt I had to dish on Victory Piggot was that he didn't like dogs very much. In an interview on March 21st, 1869, for the *Rotherby and Woodford Herald*, he'd been quoted as saying they were "slavish beasts" who were "foul germ-carriers of the worst kind."

Maybe Victory Piggot was murdered by a really angry poodle.

"What do you have?" I asked Norris.

"Hmm?" he mumbled, spilling crumbs from the plate of Oreos Mom had left outside the door when she'd gone to bed.

"Found anything?" I tried again.

"Oh yeah, look at this game," he said, turning his laptop to face me. On the screen, there was an animation of an old-fashioned classroom with a stern teacher writing questions on a blackboard.

"If you get a question wrong, you move back a row," Norris went on enthusiastically. "Then if you get the next one wrong, you have to sit in the corner with a dunce's cap. And if you get three wrong in a row, you get the cane. Cool, huh?"

"No, it's stupid. We're supposed to be looking for something to use against Victory Piggot."

"I did. There wasn't anything. How about you?" Norris asked, and then typed in *1861*. The computer pinged and the teacher beckoned the virtual Norris to come forward.

"Top of the class!" Norris yelled, upsetting his giant tub of caramel popcorn.

"Piggot didn't like dogs," I said, when Norris remembered he'd just asked me a question.

"Told you! Nothing," Norris went on cheerfully. "This was good, though." Norris dragged himself away from the game and pulled up something from the bottom of the screen. It was an old drawing of a building with the names *Deakin, Prosper, and Flack* at the top.

"What's so good about it?" I asked.

"It's the architect's drawings for Woodford School. The original building. See the date down there? 1848. And look, do you recognize that?"

I crunched across the popcorn and took a closer look. There was a sketch of some kind of lift between the storerooms in the basement and the kitchen above. It looked very familiar.

"The dumbwaiter."

Norris nodded. The dumbwaiter was one of the main reasons we'd managed to defeat the evil Mr. Jones.

"What's that?" I asked, pointing to a smallish room with lots of writing in the middle. It was farther along the hallway from the old storeroom, which was now Ms. Briars's still slightly damp drama studio.

"Let's see," Norris said, zooming in. "Principal's Study," he read.

"What's in there now?" I asked.

Norris shrugged. People only went down to the basement floor and the drama studio if they had drama, and even then they tried not to. It was one of those halls that didn't exactly encourage you to go any farther down it than you had to. It was narrow and cold and damp. And there was some sort of stupid ghost story about it.

I realized that Norris was watching me.

"I dare you," he said.

Sunday, January 27th

Punch the Clock Day

Presumably followed by Buy a New Clock Day

I didn't have a good night.

Norris bets it's because I was thinking about having to go down into the creepy hallway at school on Monday. I told him it was because he snored so much I thought somebody was trying to drill a hole in my head.

I was in a bad enough mood at breakfast without my dad going on and on about how great it must be having a new school newspaper. Mr. Chattersly put *Woodford Now and When* up on the school website so that parents can read it too.

Every time Dad said how it must be a nice change from that awful Jonny Jakes, Norris nodded his head in agreement. He could barely control himself when Dad went on about how stupid Jonny's parents must be, and how he'd have worked out what his kid was up to months ago.

Sometimes I wonder if I'm adopted.

 Monday, January 28th

I met Norris outside the drama studio at lunch. He looked almost as scared as me.

We didn't say a word as we started down the hallway. It wasn't too bad at first. The light outside the drama studio carried a few feet along, but gradually our shadows started lengthening. We made a left turn and then a right turn, and then the light was all but gone. I pulled a headlamp from my bag and put it on.

It looked like nobody had been here for a long time.

The hall was restricted to students. Judging from the thick layer of dust on the floor and all the cobwebs, the custodian had left it alone too. If that wasn't creepy enough, the temperature was falling with every step we took.

I did my best not to think about the ghost story.

I tried really hard not to remember that it was about Mrs. Guthrie, the old school nurse who used to work down here, and about how, one winter, she got a terrible fever from the kids she looked after.

When that didn't work, I started biting the inside of my cheek to try to stop myself from thinking about how she was supposed to have died a horrible and agonizing death, screaming for someone to help her.

And when that didn't work, I tried to remember the cheat code to skip up to level six on *Cold Command* so that I wouldn't start imagining her sickly yellow spirit creeping up behind me.

But it was hopeless. When Vanessa Ford had told me the story in Mrs. Henrik's biology class, it had been about as scary as a fake spider. In the hall, I could feel Mrs. Guthrie's breath on the back of my neck.

Norris had a printout of the architect's drawing in front of him. We passed some doors, which he counted. Then he stopped in front of a large, black door and nodded.

He put his hand on the door.

"That's weird," he whispered.

"What is?" I whispered back.

"The door. It's metal."

"Why's that weird?"

"How many inside doors do you know of that are made out of metal?"

I thought about it for a second. I could only think of ones that I'd seen in movies.

They usually had something very bad behind them.

Norris gave the door a push, but it was locked.

I bent down to take a closer look. Ever since we'd been locked in the drama studio last semester, I'd taken steps to keep it from happening again. I'd learned the art of lock picking through a variety of very helpful websites. It was nice to have something to take my mind off being followed by a ghost.

"Solid cast iron ring lock with keep," I muttered to myself.

"If you say so," said Norris.

I pulled out my slimline GN744 Lock Pick from my back pocket. The picks looked like mini instruments of torture as I slid them into the keyhole. It took a few minutes to get the feel of the lock, then a few more and a big spray of WD-40 to get the thing to move.

When I was done, I wiped my hands and lifted the latch above the lock. The door screeched open. We froze as the horrible sound rang around the hallway. If there really was a ghost, we'd just woken her up.

I shone my light all around the room. It was like it had been frozen in time. There was a big, heavy desk, a fireplace with a coal bucket and poker next to it, some old-fashioned cupboards, and enough cobwebs to catch about a billion flies.

We went in.

We tried to move carefully, but every step created a big puff of dust. I felt like I'd broken into a tomb.

I pulled at the cobwebs to see what was behind them, and they stuck to my shirt. Norris did the same. In a few seconds, we looked like something out of *ZombieKILLaz 4*.

The desk was clear and so were the drawers. Norris opened a wooden cabinet and found some empty glass bottles and things that kind of looked like test tubes.

I remembered that Victory Piggot was a pretty enthusiastic scientist, and I had an image of a mad professor cooking up potions in his laboratory.

It wasn't a particularly helpful image to have in the creepy, cobwebby office of a nineteenth century principal who had mysteriously disappeared.

On the far wall, there was an old painting. It was of some big old boring house, and it was hanging at an angle. For some reason, I reached out my hand and straightened it.

As soon as I touched the painting, it crashed to the floor. The cord that had held it up was completely rotten. I shut my eyes as another plume of dust filled the room. When the dust died down, I carefully opened my eyes again.

I'd just discovered where Victory Piggot kept his safe.

It was locked. I wiped the front of it with my sleeve. There was a dial with lots of numbers. I had a rough idea that you needed to listen carefully to the clicks as you turned the dial left and right so that you could tell when each part of the lock mechanism was lined up and ready to open.

Norris had a less complicated idea.

"We just need to wedge something in the side of the door and smack it a good one. Perfect!" he said as he pulled the big metal poker out of the bucket by the fireplace. "Now we need something heavy to hit it with."

We looked around for something we could use as a hammer. There was a big fat blob of cobwebs on the mantelpiece above the fire. I pulled at them and saw a glimmer of something white beneath them. When I ripped a few more webs off, I saw an eye looking back at me.

"Oh, man! I just found a skull!" I yelled, backing away in disgust.

"Cool!" Norris said, genuinely excited.

"It's not cool, it's disgusting! It used to be someone's head!" I pointed out. "And it's still got an eye!"

"That's not a skull," Norris said, looking closer. "That's a bust of someone's head. It's just what we need."

"Something pretending to be a skull is not just what we need!"

"I mean, it's just what we need to hit the poker with," Norris clarified as he cleaned the rest of the cobwebs off. "Look, it's Piggot."

Sure enough, Norris was holding the white, stony face of Woodford School's first principal in his huge, grubby hands.

Victory Piggot didn't look very happy about it.

"Put the poker in there and hold it still," Norris said as he held the top of the head in his right hand and the base with his left and lined up the hit. I jammed the poker into the crack between the door and the casing and hoped Norris wouldn't miss.

The door gave up on the fourth attack. It buckled enough so that, with a little persuasion from the poker, Norris was able to reach in a hand.

"Feels like a book," Norris said, forcing the gap open wider with his huge forearm. "Almost got it."

He carefully pulled out a small, leather-bound book. It had been protected from the dust, so it was easy to read the name on the front in bright gold lettering:

Robert Jennings

Norris was about to open the book, but he was interrupted by a fit of violent coughing. I wouldn't have minded, but it wasn't him coughing. It was someone else.

Someone else in the haunted hallway.

I switched my headlamp off and caught a glimpse of a ghostly yellowish light on the wall outside the office.

I have never stayed so still in my whole life.

The light vanished. As it did, there was the faint sound of shuffling feet, and I thought I could hear the sound of someone, or something, trying to hold back another cough.

We stayed frozen to the spot for what felt like forever. Neither of us dared to move until the shuffling sounds grew fainter and eventually disappeared. Then, as if from another world, we heard the bell ring for the end of lunch. We didn't say a word, didn't even look at each other, as we went all the way back up the stairs.

Once we were on the first floor, we did our best to brush the cobwebs off each other and blend back in to everyday school life.

It would've worked much better if we hadn't been an hour late for fifth period and walked into Mad Mean Mr. Sheen's Advanced Calculus class by mistake.

Tuesday, January 29th

Some days, the biggest excitement is trying to figure out what the little green things are in your spaghetti.

Then there are days like today.

I called Norris first thing this morning. I'd made him promise not to open the book without me. We didn't manage to look at it last night because he'd had football practice after school, and Mom had forced me to tidy up my room.

Next time Norris comes over for a sleepover, I'm going to make him wear a bib.

We met up at the park on the way to school. Norris pulled the book out of his backpack. He'd wrapped it up in a plastic bag for protection. There was a green sort of ribbon holding the book closed. I realized my hands were sweating as Norris handed over the book for me to open.

So, my readers wanted history? I'd give them history.

And Hari Patel was about to become part of it.

I gently pulled off the ribbon, opened the book to the first page, and read the first sentence aloud. It said that the book was:

The diary of Robert Fenwick Jennings

It was a slow start, but the second sentence was a bit more interesting.

For the future well-being of all mankind, please
DO NOT OPEN THIS BOTTLE.

I was about to turn the page when Norris nudged me with his elbow. He nodded across to the far side of the street. Hari Patel and Julie Singh were walking toward us. They were deep in conversation. There was no way I was going to let them get a hold of the diary, so I slipped the book back to Norris, and we headed off to school before we were spotted.

The future of mankind was going to have to wait until recess.

I could tell we were in trouble as soon as we got to homeroom. It's never a good sign when three teachers want to speak to you.

"Those two," Mr. Sheen said, pointing his bony finger at me and Norris.

"Thank you, Mr. Sheen, I'll take it from here," said Mr. Chattersly. "Please mark the boys present, Mrs. McKeane. This way, you two."

Mr. Chattersly paraded us to his office.

"Sit down," he instructed when we got there. Me and Norris sank into the two deep leather chairs facing Mr. Chattersly's desk.

"Not on the chairs," Mr. Chattersly added, pointing to the floor.

As I strained my neck to try to see over the top of his desk, Mr. Chattersly pulled up something on his computer screen.

"Boys, you've upset Mr. Sheen."

I opened my mouth to explain that everybody upsets Mr. Sheen, but Mr. Chattersly held up his hand to stop me.

"Now, I know that Mr. Sheen has, shall we say, a particular interest in upholding some of the more old-fashioned rules of the school," he said, choosing his words carefully. "But on this occasion, he has a very good point. Indeed, several points."

Mr. Chattersly skimmed what was on the screen.

"Yesterday you rudely burst into his classroom at two twenty-eight, claiming that you thought it was fifth period. Which, as you well know, finishes at one fifteen. Mr. Sheen says that your state of dress was appalling. Top buttons were undone, your ties were covered in cobwebs, and, in his own words, you 'smelled even worse than most sixth graders.'

"Worst of all, he says that you were obviously lying when he asked you where you had been all that time. Or can you prove," said Mr. Chattersly, looking meaningfully at us and then back at the computer screen, "that 'Mrs. Gelt asked you to help her with her chemistry demonstration on flammable oxides, but it got a little out of hand'?"

I shot Norris an angry look. That's the last time I let him try to talk us out of trouble.

"Do you have anything to say for yourselves?" Mr. Chattersly asked.

We shook our heads.

"I thought as much. I take this matter seriously, boys. Missing class is bad enough, but attempting to deceive a teacher in such a blatant fashion is very troubling.

You will spend the rest of the day in my office completing the work that your teachers have been kind enough to leave you. Mrs. Singh will contact your parents and ask them to come in to discuss the matter with me this afternoon. Understood?"

We nodded.

For a second, I wondered if it was a good time to mention Robert Jennings's warning, but Mr. Chattersly didn't exactly look like he was in the mood for letting us wander downstairs for another look in Victory Piggot's safe.

Instead, me and Norris worked in silence as Mr. Chattersly tapped away on his computer keyboard. I tried to catch a reflection of the computer screen in his glasses, but I could only read the title:

```
           Victory Piggot:
 A Special Assembly For A Special Man
```

He was going to give the speech that afternoon. At least we were going to miss it.

After an hour, I was still struggling with the French homework from Madame Le Blanc. The first task was to translate the instructions, but I was pretty sure she didn't want me to bake my horse in the garden.

My brain was saved from a total meltdown by a knock on Mr. Chattersly's door.

"Come," Mr. Chattersly commanded.

One day, I want to boss people around like that.

"Sorry to bother you, Mr. Chattersly," Mrs. Singh said as she stuck her head around the door. "I've called both sets of parents, and they're happy to come in at two o'clock. Well, when I say happy . . ."

Mr. Chattersly smiled. "I know what you mean, Mrs. Singh. Is there anything else?"

"No. Yes. Hang on. What did you want again, dear?" Mrs. Singh said, sticking her head back out into the hall and speaking to someone we couldn't see. "Oh yes, and Hari Patel would like to have a quick word. He says it's important."

At the mention of Hari's name, Mr. Chattersly was all smiles.

"Well, if Hari says it's important, it probably is. Tell him I'm coming."

Mr. Chattersly locked his computer screen and pulled his suit jacket on. As he left, he gave us a hard stare.

"What do you think we should do?" I asked Norris.

"I think we're supposed to describe where we live."

"Not about the French homework, you idiot! About the possible threat to mankind."

Norris shrugged. "What can we do? We're stuck in here until our parents arrive. Then they'll ground us forever."

"Not during assembly. We could sneak out and then check the safe. We have to find out what's in the bottle. You read what Jennings said."

"But there wasn't a bottle."

"Look, it was dark, it was creepy, and you only had your hand in that safe for a few seconds. You can't be sure. Get the book out. Let's see if it says anything more about it. If it's just Robert Jennings's idea of a joke, maybe it will say so. I'll keep an eye on the door."

Norris thought about it for a second, and then pulled the book out of his backpack again. He flipped to the second page and quietly read it out loud.

If you have discovered this diary and this bottle, then my plan has failed and the future of all God's creatures now rests in your hands. Please, whoever you are, do that which I dared not. Destroy this bottle and its foul contents!

Again, I beg of you, friend, whatever you do,

DO NOT OPEN THIS BOTTLE.

RFJ

I looked at Norris. He looked back.

"Well?" I asked.

"You have to admit he's consistent," Norris replied.

Norris was about to turn the page when I heard Mr. Chattersly say a cheerful goodbye to Hari.

Norris tucked the book away just in time.

When he came back, Mr. Chattersly worked us hard. No talking. No snacks. No bathroom breaks. It was torture.

And wondering what Robert Jennings was talking about was doing nothing for my ability to remember how you say "the most boring place on earth" in French.

At lunch, Mr. Chattersly asked what we wanted. We put in an order with Mrs. Singh for pizza, chicken nuggets, and fries. But Mr. Chattersly is on a healthy food streak, so we ended up with something that looked like a lawnmower had been emptied on a plate.

When it was nearly two o'clock, Mr. Chattersly stopped typing up his speech and printed it off. He looked pleased with himself. Before he left, he gave us a full-blown lecture about what would happen if we so much as breathed the wrong way while he was gone.

I might've even paid attention if he hadn't had a booger flapping in and out of his nose when he shouted.

When he'd finally left us in peace, we counted to sixty before we made our move. The coast was clear, so we ran all the way back to Piggot's office.

The big door creaked open. It was pitch black inside, and we didn't have time to get flashlights, so we had to feel our way across the room. Norris tripped over something on the floor. The next second, an invisible dust cloud hit us. In the dark, we'd forgotten to hold our breaths.

I'm not sure my lungs will ever forgive me.

When the hacking and retching and eye-wiping finally died down, Norris went back to heading toward the safe.

"Anything?" I whispered when I figured he'd finally gotten there.

"Nothing," came the reply out of the darkness.

"Are you sure?"

"Hang on, there's a piece of paper."

"Bring it out so we can see it."

We took a deep breath and stumbled out of the office into the hall. When we had enough light to see our feet again, Norris unfolded the slip of paper.

We could just make out what it said:

> ### Dear Jonny Jakes,
>
> I'm guessing it was you. Thanks for letting me in — I've been wondering what to do about that door for a while! It was very kind of you to open the safe too.
>
> I can't wait to find out what this stuff actually does.
>
> Hari
>
> P.S. Mr. Chattersly is <u>particularly excited!</u>

"I've got a bad feeling about Mr. Chattersly's special assembly," I said.

Norris nodded.

We crept carefully through the double doors at the back of the auditorium. There was still a chance that nothing was going to happen, so we had to be ready to book it back to Mr. Chattersly's office without being noticed.

It was soon obvious that something was up, though. You could tell by the way nobody had fallen asleep.

From the back of the auditorium, I could just see that Mr. Chattersly had a small table next to him on the stage. On it was a small bottle.

Keeping our heads down, me and Norris nudged our way closer.

We stopped a couple of rows from the front, and I pulled my spy telescope out of my pocket. It looks just like a pen. I put it to my eye and adjusted the focus.

The writing on the bottle's label was fancy and loopy, like the writing in Robert Jennings's diary. What it said was just as interesting.

I gave Norris the telescope to make sure I wasn't seeing things. His jaw dropped open.

I began to register what Mr. Chattersly was saying.

"Of course, it's all complete nonsense." He chuckled. "The

Behold the
Holy Grail!

He who drinks
this elixir
will have

EVERLASTING
LIFE!

quest for the Holy Grail has fascinated people for centuries, and dear old Victory Piggot is just another mere mortal obsessed with the idea of eternal life. And so, to put my money where my mouth is, and to prove that you shouldn't always take your principal too seriously, I am going to drink what's in this bottle. After all," he added, flicking his hair and winking, "if I'm wrong, what's the worst that can happen?"

Everyone laughed.

A cold sweat broke out on the back of my neck. I realized that Norris wasn't next to me anymore. I looked to see where he'd gone. He was pushing his way to the steps at the side of the stage.

Mr. Chattersly picked up the ancient bottle. He was loving all the attention and turned to pose with it for Hari, who was taking his picture for another front page.

Norris had made it onto the steps, but all eyes were on Mr. Chattersly, who was pulling the cork out of the bottle.

"Cheers!" he said as Norris pounded, still unnoticed, toward him.

Just as the bottle touched Mr. Chattersly's lips, he paused. His smile had vanished, and through the telescope, I could see that his hand was shaking slightly.

Maybe it was a dramatic pause. Maybe it was second thoughts. I'll never know, because my view was suddenly obscured by Norris flying through the air screaming "NOOOO!" at the top of his lungs and football tackling Mr. Chattersly to the floor.

In a split second, the mood turned from excitement to terror. Everyone was stunned, and a few people couldn't stop shrieking. Norris got to his knees and stared at the crumpled figure he'd left on the floor. He looked like he couldn't believe what he'd done.

The whole auditorium held its breath and waited to see if Norris had just killed their principal.

Eventually, a low groan came from the heap on the floor. With one hand rubbing his head, Mr. Chattersly sat up. In the other hand, he was still clutching the bottle. It hadn't been smashed, and amazingly it still looked almost full.

Norris heaved a sigh of relief.

Suddenly Mr. Chattersly's free hand started to clutch at his throat. His eyes bulged and watered, and he started shaking like someone having a fit. One of the teachers rushed forward and grabbed the bottle out of his hand.

Norris tried to hide behind the table.

As quickly as it had started, Mr. Chattersly's shaking

stopped. His eyes stopped bulging and his shoulders relaxed. He started patting himself all over as if he was checking to see if he was still there. He flapped his ears back and forth, stretched his mouth open, and flicked his tongue up and down. Then he opened and shut his eyes repeatedly.

Satisfied that his face worked, he got to his feet. He looked down at them for a while, like he hadn't seen them before. Then he inspected his hands. He put one of them in front of his mouth and breathed on it. A large grin spread across his face.

Then he looked at us.

"What are you all staring at?" he bellowed.

Everyone in the auditorium wondered if their ears were playing tricks on them. It wasn't just because it wasn't the kind of thing Mr. Chattersly usually said. It wasn't even because he was acting so aggressive all of a sudden.

It was because Mr. Chattersly didn't sound anything like Mr. Chattersly.

"And what on earth are you all wearing? And what —"

Suddenly Mr Chattersly's whole body shook, and there was a gigantic gasp as Mr. Chattersly's voice changed back to its normal, less ear-shredding tone.

"Um, hi. Alistair Chattersly, pleased to meet you," he said.

To himself.

His body shook again.

"Alistair Chattersly? What kind of ridiculous name is that?" the booming voice answered. "Where's Robert?"

"Which one?"

"My assistant, you gibbering fool!"

"Uh, well, Robert Preston is on the school council," the original voice of Mr. Chattersly informed himself. "Give our visitor a little wave, Robert, so he can see who you are."

Robert Preston couldn't have looked more confused if someone had smacked him on the head with a wet fish and asked him what ice cream he wanted with his fries. In the end, he decided it was probably best to give Mr. Chattersly a little wave.

"You're not Robert, you insolent boy! Report to my office immediately!" Mr. Chattersly thundered before looking around the auditorium as if he'd never seen the place before. "What have you done with it?"

Mr. Chattersly shook violently again.

"There's nothing to be worried about, children," the usual voice of Mr. Chattersly said as calmly as it could manage. "But it seems like our little experiment has gone slightly wrong."

"I couldn't agree more!" the loud voice agreed. "You, sir, have the mind of an imbecile, the hair of a woman, and what have you done to my school? It looks abominable!"

"Ah, well, you see, there are bound to have been some changes. After all, it is the twenty-first century."

Mr. Chattersly shook one final time and took in his surroundings with an expression of great distaste.

"We'll see about that!" he bellowed, and stormed off.

When we'd recovered from the shock, me and Norris raced back to Mr. Chattersly's office, working under the assumption that at least some of him might've remembered about us.

When we got there, we quickly pulled out a few books and pretended to work.

It was a few minutes before Mr. Chattersly appeared. He was still arguing with himself as he came in. Apparently someone had dropped a packet of chips on the stairs.

"It's a disgrace! I want the culprits identified and punished immediately! Where do you keep your cane?"

"I'm afraid we don't do things like that anymore."

"What are you twittering on about, you dim-witted fool? You mean to say you don't beat the students? How on earth do you maintain discipline?"

"Well, we have a more collaborative approach. Of course there's detention, but we prefer to talk to the kids and try to make them understand what they've done wrong."

"A throbbing backside lets them know perfectly well when they've done something wrong and . . ."

Mr. Chattersly had realized that he wasn't alone in his office. He glared at us fiercely, and I had no doubt about what half of him wanted to do to us.

Luckily, the other half slid back into place.

"Ah, yes. You two. I think, under the circumstances, we'll skip the talk with your parents. They will, however, take you home immediately, and this will be marked down on your school record as a half-day suspension for rude behavior and an unforgivable lapse in punctuality. Now run along."

We rushed out the door just as Mr. Chattersly's more violent side returned and started looking around for something to hit us with.

After Mrs. Singh explained that Mr. Chattersly was unavoidably detained, my parents drove me home in silence. I got sent to my room without any after-school snack. My dad said he wasn't going to talk to me until I'd had time to think very carefully about what I'd done.

It was the best news I'd had all day.

Wednesday, January 30th

My parents still aren't talking to me. I think they're trying to show how disappointed they are. And I don't think Norris will be welcome for another sleepover anytime soon. Mom passed me a note over breakfast saying I was to have nothing to do with him for the rest of the week.

When I met him at the park, Norris told me his parents had said the same.

He had big bags under his eyes. His mom had made him turn his lights out early, so he'd had to wait for his parents to go to sleep before he could get started on the diary.

I asked him how it was. He said it was pretty boring at first, but it got going after a while, and that when I got to the part titled "How to Safely Turn Living Tissue into Viable Fluids," I'd probably throw up. He figured Mr. Chattersly was now half Mr. Chattersly and half Victory Piggot.

I said I'd already figured that out on my own, but why was that such a bad thing for the future of all God's creatures? He gave me the diary and told me to find out for myself.

Hari has put out another issue of *Woodford Now and When*.

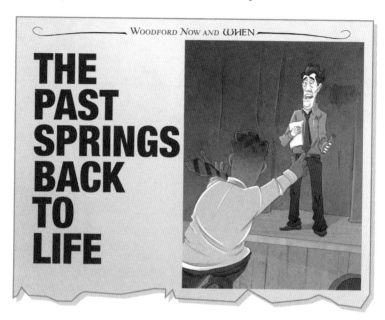

He managed to get a brief interview with our half-new principal, but it was cut short when the Victory Piggot part of him apparently threatened to pull Hari's liver out through his throat if he didn't stop poking his nose where it didn't belong.

It's been a strange day. Mr. Chattersly/Victory Piggot have pretty much stayed in his/their office trying to sort out his/their/its difference(s). No one knows what's going to happen next, and I have absolutely no idea what the correct use of pronouns is in this situation.

Everyone realizes that drinking from the bottle did something really weird to Mr. Chattersly, but there've been a lot of arguments about exactly what it was. Everyone who believes in ghosts is telling everyone who doesn't they told them so. Everyone who doesn't believe in ghosts is telling everyone who does to shut up while they try to come up with a better explanation.

There are some pretty smug believers in the supernatural out there.

Thursday, January 31st

It's stupid o'clock.

I've been reading Robert Jennings's diary and I can't sleep. I now know two very important things:

1. Victory Piggot is definitely alive and well over one hundred years after his mysterious disappearance.

2. He's completely nuts.

Looks like I have a new enemy.

The diary started out kind of confusingly. The first two pages, the ones I'd already seen, had obviously been written after everything else. Once you got past those, the diary began explaining it all from the very beginning.

Like Norris said, it was pretty boring at first. Robert Jennings had really small handwriting and kept using words like *forthwith*. It made my head hurt, but I kept going.

He enrolled at Woodford School in 1865. His dad had sent him because he wanted his son to be *at the forefront of the great scientific age* and figured Victory Piggot was exactly what his son needed. He told Robert to work hard.

At first, Robert was totally obedient. He wrote that he was *most eager to please both my father and the illustrious Woodford principal*. It got worse. Soon he was saying stuff like *Mr. Piggot held our minds firmly in his grasp* and *Once again, Mr. Piggot shone light where before there were only shadows*.

I almost had to get a bucket.

Although he was really strict with the other boys, for some reason Victory Piggot went easy on Robert. There seemed to be some kind of bond between them. Piggot only caned him once, and even then, Robert said, *the strokes fell lightly*. Maybe it was because Piggot wanted someone to *further discuss his fascinating philosophy* with, or maybe it was because Robert was a big weirdo.

Either way, when he was *invited to assist the principal in his own private research*, Robert Jennings was a seriously happy camper.

After a hard day's corporal punishment, Piggot liked nothing more than telling Robert about how they were living in a *Golden Age of Discovery*. There was a bunch of science stuff about microscopes and bacteria that I didn't really get. Then he ranted about *cursed foreigners* like *Robert Koch and Louis Pasteur meddling where they didn't belong*. Apparently those guys were figuring out how germs carried diseases and were generally trying to turn the world into a healthier place.

Piggot insisted that if the world really wanted to know how diseases worked, it was going to be Victory Piggot who told them.

He asked Robert if he wanted to help him with his work. Robert replied that he would be *delighted and honored to have the privilege of pursuing so noble a purpose.*

Soon Robert was hard at work in the laboratory putting horrible things in animals to see what would happen to them.

Basically, they died.

There's a lot more detail in the diary, but if you don't have a mop handy, it's probably best not to go into it.

One day Victory Piggot was super excited. He invited Robert into his office to show him why.

It was a great honor to be invited into the principal's office. Normally, boys are only allowed to enter for reasons of punishment. I thought of how proud my father would be if he could have seen me.

About the shelves Mr. Piggot had arranged an impressive collection of jars and so forth.

The labels were in Mr. Piggot's own fine hand, but he used symbols and shorthand that, in my ignorance, I could only guess at.

In a state of much excitement, Mr. Piggot pulled down two of these jars and then, from beneath his desk, two small cages. In one cage was a rabbit, in the other a wren.

"Watch this," he cried, eyes sparkling.

Into the rabbit's cage he placed a lettuce leaf. The rabbit, on spying the leaf, set to it in vigorous fashion. Then a spider was placed in the wren's cage and the bird responded likewise.

"You see?" Mr. Piggot inquired, with such enthusiasm and beads of excited perspiration on his brow that I wondered if he had temporarily lost control of his faculties.

After all, I had only seen a rabbit eating a lettuce leaf and a wren eating a spider, and what was so remarkable about that?

"Yes sir, I see," I replied, not knowing quite what else to do.

Mr. Piggot sensed my predicament.

"Be patient, Robert. The best is yet to come."

Mr. Piggot picked up the jar on his right and drew a syringe full of the dark liquid therein; this he injected into the rabbit. He repeated the procedure with the liquid in the jar on his left, only this was injected into the wren.

At first, both animals seemed unaffected by the experience, but then I noticed that the rabbit was less and less concerned with the lettuce leaf and the wren less and less concerned with devouring the spider.

I shall never forget the bird stopping, mid-meal, with three hairy legs still hanging out of the side of its beak.

Mr. Piggot then brought out another lettuce leaf and another spider, only this time the rabbit got the spider and the wren the lettuce leaf. In an instant, both of the creatures' appetites were restored and I was left very much amazed.

Somehow, Victory Piggot had made an amazing breakthrough. Through researching the transfer of germs, he had also learned how to transfer behavior from one animal to another.

From that day on, Robert Jennings was put to work swapping all kinds of animal behavior: sparrows tried to dig a nest in the ground, rats thought they could lay eggs, and frogs tried to fly. There was usually a lot of cleaning up afterward.

For a couple of years, Robert Jennings and Victory Piggot were like the sorcerer and his apprentice, and everything was good.

Well . . . not for the animals, obviously.

Then things started to change. Piggot got more secretive. He spent less time roaming the school looking for excuses to hurt people. Robert was invited into Piggot's office less and less. When he was allowed in, he noticed that the labeling system, which he'd finally gotten the hang of, had changed again. There were symbols and equations that he couldn't find in any of the regular textbooks and that his master was reluctant to explain.

The animals changed too. Instead of mice and frogs and birds, Piggot was keeping larger animals. Cats and dogs stared mournfully out of their cages.

Then, on November 23rd, 1869, Robert Jennings seriously freaked out. I don't blame him.

A morning I will never forget.

Master Spencer was conducting a review of our Latin vocabulary, as was the custom on a Friday. My mind, I confess, was wandering as he conjugated the verb "morir" for what felt like the umpteenth time. Instead of chanting back, I was gazing through the window, listening to the whistle of a robin as it enjoyed its freedom beyond my gloomy classroom.

The pleasant birdsong was suddenly interrupted by the clamor of a dog's bark.

I wondered what had caused the dog to bark and which of the town's remaining mongrels the offending noise belonged to. There has been a stir in the local newspaper recently about a number of household pets that have gone missing, and the sound of a dog barking has become something of a rarity.

My thoughts were interrupted by a sharp elbow in my ribs. I turned in my chair to protest my neighbor's actions, but all thoughts of revenge were banished when I saw Peter Spencer and realized that the barking was not, after all, coming from without.

It was coming from him.

It was not thirty seconds later when class was interrupted by the appearance of Mr. Piggot. His face was flushed and red from exertion and, I believe, a sense of panic. Peter was swiftly removed by means of his ear lobe, and we were told to get on with our work and immediately dispel the boy's foolishness from our minds.

In that moment, Robert realized why Piggot had been keeping so quiet. His classmates may have thought that Peter Spencer had just been goofing off, but Robert knew differently.

He knew that Victory Piggot was no longer just trying his experiments out on animals.

Peter Spencer was rarely seen again. The boys were told he had a tropical fever and needed to be confined to his bed. One time, Robert said he was allowed down to breakfast and *appeared to be his normal self again.*

Then he peed on a table leg.

Robert noticed changes in the other boys. Edward Knight's limp kept swapping legs. Benjamin Hines, the worst mathematician at the school, finally learned his multiplication tables — overnight. And Henry Dent, a boy who *couldn't be trusted to put his trousers on right-side up,* one day amazed everyone by *catching an absolute snorker at second slip.* Apparently that's a really good thing in cricket.

This kind of thing went on for a year. During school breaks, Robert tried to explain what was going on to his father, but he took no notice. Robert started complaining that his father didn't understand him and that all his parents were interested in was whether he was doing all right in school.

Finally he was speaking my language.

It was in his final year that Robert was once again invited in to Piggot's office. He didn't want to go, but he knew he had no choice. Besides, he had made his mind up that Piggot couldn't be allowed to continue, and it was up to him to stop the principal.

On entering the office, I was relieved to see that there were no longer any cages harboring those poor, unfortunate creatures. My guard was up, though, the moment Mr. Piggot turned to face me.

Even since the end of last semester, his appearance had changed dramatically. His features had become pinched and lined, and his eyes held a special light only to be found in those in a high attitude of fear, desperation, or lunacy.

"Ah, Robert. I have neglected you, I know. But the demands of progress have to be met! And Robert, I have made much progress!"

These last words were said with such a manic conviction that I could feel the hairs rise up on the back of my neck. Every natural urge in my body was telling me to leave this madman alone, but I knew I could only defeat him if he still believed he had my confidence.

I beseeched him to inform me further and did my utmost to once again play the part of the eager apprentice.

"Patience, Robert. I know you desire to know more and you shall not be disappointed, but there are a few more steps I must take. Steps I must take alone. Attend on me at this hour, on this day, a month from now, and your faith in me shall have its just reward."

So that's what Robert did.

If you just had something to eat, I suggest you read this next part later.

I returned to Mr. Piggot's office exactly one month later, as he had bid me do. As I knocked on the door, I prepared my features so that my feelings of disgust and revulsion should once again be hidden by a mask of feigned interest.

At first my knocking received no reply, so after a polite pause, I tried again. This time the familiar voice replied.

"Is that Robert?"

I assured him that it was.

"Are you alone?"

Again I answered yes. Then the voice boomed once more.

"Come."

For a few moments after I opened the door, I was unable to distinguish anything in the room I had just entered. The first shapes that came out of the gloom were those of the desk and chair. Then gradually I began to make out the form of Mr. Piggot. His white, whiskery sideburns seemed to be floating in the blackness.

I stood before the silent figure, more scared than I have ever been before, but more determined than ever that whatever the monster in front of me was planning to do, it must be stopped tonight.

An oil lamp on the desk flickered to life. It was painful to my eyes, having just become accustomed to the dark. When I could see clearly again, I noticed that although the light reached me, some sort of shield behind the lamp was preventing the light from falling on Mr. Piggot, so that he remained an outline only.

I could feel myself being inspected.

"I'm sorry about all this, Robert, but you will soon see why I have to be so sure. You are about to become the beneficiary of all my years of research. If you do exactly as I say, in a matter of minutes you will become the most famous, the most celebrated man to have ever lived.

"My dear boy, you will live forever."

I had no reply to give to this. What reply could there be?

"It is time," the dark shape commanded. "Listen carefully, or these will be the last words you ever hear. What is about to happen will be very unpleasant. You may wish to close your eyes. But when it is over, there is one thing you must do. Do you understand me, Robert?" This last question was snapped, and there was a sense of desperation once more in Mr. Piggot's manner.

I nodded, and he appeared to be satisfied.

"In a short time, a bottle will appear in front of you. All you have to do is drink it."

I nodded again. I confess that I could not prevent myself from a small sob of fear.

"You have served me well, Robert. Do this final act for me and all will be well. I promise. Now close your eyes."

It began with a grunt and wheezy breathing, as of an old man under some horrible duress. Then, a stifled scream. Then . . . it felt as if the room itself was dissolving. In a terrible panic, I blinked open my eyes, just to make sure there was still ground for me to stand on. I regretted it soon enough.

The shape that had been my principal had become some sort of bubbling, heaving mass. It was as if a barrel of tar had somehow come to life. There were eyes, but they were liquid and fathomless. There was a neck, but it coiled and lengthened and looped until it was impossible to tell head from body, or body from head.

A terrible screech from the cavernous mouth made me shut my eyes again. And now a frothing, fermenting gurgle tormented my ears, accompanied by the foulest of stenches. I tried my hardest not to succumb to the burning sensation in my forehead and the sickening numbness everywhere else, but I did not succeed.

The last thing I remember was a fearsome whooshing sound, as if everything was being sucked from the room.

When I came to, the room swam before my eyes. As it came back into focus, I could see that the black shape behind the desk had disappeared.

In its place, bearing a strange label, was a small bottle.

Sweet dreams.

Norris didn't have to ask me if I'd read the diary. He saw the bags under my eyes and just nodded.

"So what do we do?" he asked.

"What we always do," I replied. "Tell the truth."

"What if no one believes it?"

"That's their problem."

And by the look of it, it's going to be a big problem.

Mr. Chattersly and Victory Piggot have worked out their issues. Well, Piggot has worked out his. Mr. Chattersly is going to do exactly what Piggot tells him to.

I was on my way to biology when I heard footsteps come up behind me. The next thing I knew, something heavy smacked me on the back of the head.

"That's the way to do it, Chattersly," boomed the voice of Victory Piggot. "Let them know who's in charge."

I watched with stars in my eyes as Mr. Chattersly's body marched past me. It was swinging a massive dictionary in its hand and making a bunch of eighth grade girls run for cover. Victory Piggot was in an unpleasantly good mood.

"You see that? Respect! That's what that is, Chattersly.
I'll soon have this school working properly again."

By lunchtime, I could see we didn't just need to worry
about the school being run by a violent maniac.

It's more the fact that everybody seems to like it.

"It was awesome in World Religions," George Murray
informed everyone standing next to him in the lunch
line. "Chattersly came into the room. He told everyone
to stand up and then asked them questions. He asked
me to list ten differences between Christianity and
Judaism. I only got to three, so he smacked me seven
times on the hand with a ruler. Look at the blisters
on that!"

Everyone agreed
they were very
impressive and
couldn't wait to
get some of
their own.

Hari is going to get another interview, only this time it looks like Piggot might be warming to the publicity. He told everyone in assembly that his reappearance would be fully explained to them in tomorrow's issue of *Woodford Now and When*, along with the publication of a new set of school rules.

Oh joy.

The rest of the assembly mostly involved him lecturing us about "standards," "discipline," and how we were all "sniveling little brats." It went down really well.

To finish off, he made us all sing.

He's got to go.

Friday, February 1st

It would be a lot easier to defeat Victory Piggot if I didn't feel like a total zombie. I tried to get started on the comeback issue of *The Woodford Word* last night, but I fell asleep at my laptop.

You can still see the % sign on my forehead.

I'm so tired that I can't think straight. I can't even eat right. I nearly drowned in my own cereal this morning. Mom kept asking me if there was anything wrong, but I didn't know where to start.

I was almost too tired to notice the new edition of *Woodford Now and When*. Unfortunately Norris pointed it out in homeroom. He also pointed out that Hari's interview had made it onto the front page of practically every national newspaper, along with his headline:

WOODFORD NOW AND WHEN

Two Is Better Than One

FIRST WOODFORD PRINCIPAL RETURNS TO DO HIS DUTY

In another extraordinary world first, Woodford School has found itself with a new principal. Or should we say *principals*.

The school is crawling with reporters. All the kids are desperate to be interviewed and give their opinion on what it's like to have their principal possessed by the spirit of a crazy "ye olde" guy.

It's not an opportunity that comes along very often.

Julie had another article in the paper. This time she'd written about how much better the standards of behavior were back when "children knew their place" and how Victory Piggot's influence could be a real boost to "improving youngsters' behavior."

It confirmed my long-held belief about anyone who uses the word "youngster."

The new school rules took up the rest of the paper.

Basically, you can't do anything.

The teachers are terrified of Piggot. They all try to keep out of his way. This morning he was so busy twisting Michaela Gray's ear for daring to look him in the eye that he smacked Mr. Hamilton in the face with his elbow. Mr. Hamilton apologized and said it wouldn't happen again.

Michaela Gray couldn't wait for everyone to see how red and swollen her ear lobe was.

At the end of the day, Norris wanted to know the game plan. I said that we were going to work our butts off over the weekend. In particular, we were going to make sure we let the world know that Victory Piggot was an evil mad scientist and that he shouldn't be trusted.

Norris said what about the fact that our parents still didn't want us to see each other?

I said what about it?

Saturday, February 2nd

My much-needed sleeping in was ruined by the familiar sound of Victory Piggot.

And the unbelievable hypocrisy of my parents.

Apparently it *is* okay to have the TV on and blaring first thing in the morning, *as long* as you're watching an interview with a lunatic who's demanding the death penalty for teenagers who show their underwear off in public.

I thought I was safe when my parents went shopping, but it turns out that Victory Piggot has already become a must-have brand. They came back with Victory Piggot hand towels, a Victory Piggot pencil case, a set of Victory Piggot mugs, and a Victory Piggot robe my mom bought especially for my dad. It has a picture of Victory Piggot waving a cane and looking even angrier than usual.

Dad liked it so much, he put it on right after dinner.

As if my digestive system needed any more aggravation.

Sunday, February 3rd

Me and Norris have been working on *The Woodford Word* all day. I stockpiled food yesterday and sneaked him into my room early this morning before there was any chance of meeting the Victory Piggot robe.

The only interruptions were Mom and Dad, who kept shouting for me to come downstairs. They wanted me to read all the special Victory Piggot articles in the Sunday paper.

I've stopped working twice. Once to write this and once to accidentally spill orange juice all over the Victory Piggot articles in the Sunday paper.

Monday, February 4th

The Woodford Word was back in business first thing Monday morning.

There was the headline:

THE WOODFORD WORD

THE SHAME OF VICTORY PIGGOT

Victory Piggot, the man of the moment, owes his reappearance to a dark and dreadful secret.

There was the expert witness with the in-depth inside story, exposing the secrets of Victory Piggot's gruesome past:

> *I regret to write, dear diary, that it is clear to me now that Victory Piggot is one of the most dangerous men to have ever lived.*

And, just in case the extracts from Robert Jennings's diary didn't do the trick, there were lots of pictures of fluffy animals looking sad.

Nobody likes a man who's mean to bunny rabbits.

I made sure the reporters hanging around school got a copy. Then I left a note under Mr. Bream's desk letting my fellow students know where they could get theirs. I even left a pile outside the teachers' lounge.

By nine o'clock, I expected to be sold out. By lunch, I expected a riot. By the end of the day, I expected Victory Piggot to be gone.

They say two out of three isn't bad.

But one out of three sucks.

The selling-out part wasn't a problem. Victory Piggot's name could sell a pile of pus right now. The problem is, I've made him more popular than ever.

"Have you seen this?" George Murray cried as he came into French class waving *The Woodford Word* above his head. "Piggot turned a kid into a dog!"

"Awesome!" Syfur Dravid shouted, flicking through his copy. "And look at this! He made frogs think they could actually fly."

"Suicidal frogs! Super awesome!"

"Epic!"

Syfur attempted to do an impersonation. It mostly involved him jumping off a chair going, "Ribbit! Splat!"

Over and over again.

As for the riot, most kids spent their lunch drawing pictures of mutated animals on their backpacks and working on a new set of Victory Piggot catchphrases.

Even the reporters didn't seem that bothered by Piggot's past. I heard one reporter on his cell phone. He was telling someone to mock up some pictures of mixed-up animals and blabbing on about how Victory Piggot was way ahead of his time.

The only group of people who are showing any kind of common sense are the teachers. Ironic or what? They usually avoid *The Woodford Word* like the plague, so I was surprised to see that the pile of papers outside the teachers' lounge had almost disappeared.

I'll make sure they have to pay for it next time.

The teachers might be scared of Victory Piggot, but that doesn't mean they have to like him. Ms. Briars was particularly upset. She's the completely cuckoo but surprisingly violent drama teacher who helped us defeat Mr. Jones. She gave a TV interview saying that she was worried about the "mixed moral message" students might be getting from their new principal.

Although Piggot was by no means gone, he was at least keeping a low profile. I only saw Chattersly once, on the way to history. He was muttering something to Hari, who was walking a step behind him, taking notes.

I met up with Norris at the end of school. I needed some answers.

"I don't get it. Where did we go wrong?" I asked him.

"I guess people love eccentrics," he replied.

"But he's not eccentric! He's psycho!"

"I'm not sure most people know the difference," Norris said cheerfully. It takes more than a maniac to get Norris down.

A group of seventh graders swarmed past with their arms pulled out of their coats, flapping the empty sleeves. They were doing their own flying frog impressions.

"Well, *I'm* going to have to teach them, then," I muttered, watching them pass by.

We walked on in silence. For some reason Norris had lost his smile.

About time.

As I got close to the school this morning, the mutter of angry voices drifted my way. It was strange. They sounded less like disappointed teenagers than usual.

Then I saw why. Underneath their cheap suits and bad jewelry, the teachers had gotten in touch with a part of themselves they hadn't used for a long time.

Their spines.

It wasn't just Ms. Briars who was prepared to make a stand against her new boss now. The playground was filled with teachers carrying banners. They said things like:

> # MORALS MAKETH A MAN

> # FOR UNTO WHOMSOEVER MUCH IS GIVEN, OF HIM SHALL BE MUCH REQUIRED!

Some of them even made sense.

The students were loving it. Everyone was taking pictures. The reporters who were still around were lapping it up too.

"Uh, hi."

I turned to see who had tapped me on the shoulder.

"Shouldn't you have taken some pictures?" Julie Singh nodded at the teachers, who were beginning to march back into the school. She held her hands up. "Not that I'd try to tell you how to do your job."

"I did," I replied, less angrily than I expected. "I have a camera here . . ." I pointed at the button camera on my shirt. "It looks just like a button," I added.

Julie nodded. I waited for the "told you so" or at least some mention of *TWW*'s recent epic fail. For some reason it didn't arrive. Julie just stared at the button camera. I couldn't think of anything else to do, so I tried to stare at it too.

All the moment needed was someone to say "awkward."

At recess, the teachers were at it again. Their chants were growing bolder.

"Piggot, Piggot, Piggot, you really should think carefully about what you've done," squeaked the nervous chemistry teacher whose name everyone forgot.

"Victory P isn't for me!" called out Mr. Grieve, impressed with his rhyme.

"Piggot! Piggot! Piggot! Out! Out! Out!" yelled Ms. Briars in full flow.

It was a beautiful scene, and it got even prettier when Mr. Chattersly/Victory Piggot was forced to come out. Instantly a bunch of microphones were thrust in his face. He did his best to act like he wasn't bothered by all the fuss, but his forehead was tense and his eyes looked tired.

"All right, all right, you've made your point!" Mr. Chattersly said, back in his normal voice. It sounded quiet and strange.

"Piggot! Piggot! Piggot! Out! Out! Out!" the teachers replied.

Mr. Chattersly had to increase his volume.

"All right! I can hear you! Mr. Piggot has agreed to talk to you all in the teachers' lounge at the end of the day. But only if you go back to your classes now!"

The teachers huddled together and did a bit of mumbling. Ms. Briars found herself nudged to the front.

"And has he decided to leave?" she asked.

Mr. Chattersly squirmed and tried to control his inner Piggot. Hari whispered in his ear.

"He has decided to consider his position," Mr. Chattersly told the mob.

The teachers muttered briefly among themselves again.

"All right," Ms. Briars said, looking Mr. Chattersly squarely in the eye. "As long as he considers it very carefully."

It was a weird afternoon. No one really knew what to do. Bells rang. Kids shuffled in and out of classrooms. Teachers talked.

Everyone watched the clock.

At 3:30 p.m., the bell rang for the end of the day, but no one was ready to go home. The teachers descended on the teachers' lounge while the kids and reporters waited outside and tried to figure out ways of listening to what was being said behind the closed doors. It mostly involved going "Shh!" every two seconds.

By 4 p.m., a lot of people had given up, and the crowd in the hall was thinning. By 5 p.m., we still hadn't heard a thing. The only excitement had been the lunch ladies taking a tray of drinks and cookies in. It wasn't much to base a story on.

At 6 p.m., we gave up. It was either that or miss *Monster Truck Mash-Up*, and there was no way I was giving up my weekly fix of mechanized violence for a story about bland sugar cookies and a bunch of fruit punch.

Wednesday, February 6th

I set my alarm clock for 5:30 a.m. so that me and Norris could get into school first thing. I wanted to capture every last bit of a Piggot-free day. The plan was ruined, however, about ten seconds after 5:30 a.m., when the alarm clock was the victim of an act of violence from which it didn't recover.

My mom woke me up three hours later.

When I got to school, Norris was waiting for me at the front doors. He was looking pretty smug.

"And I thought *I* was late."

"Alarm clock malfunction," I informed him.

"You too?" he said with a grin.

"Come on."

We headed straight for the teachers' lounge, but we didn't get very far. The second we stepped into the building, the fire alarm went off.

We piled into the schoolyard along with the rest of the students and lined up with our homerooms. No one knew what the deal with Piggot was, so no one was taking any chances by messing around.

When the alarm stopped, there was a strange silence. This was usually when the teachers either took attendance, lectured you on the importance of fire safety, or did both at the same time. But all you could hear was the wind, pushing at the trees on the edge of the playground. There wasn't a teacher in sight.

The silence lingered.

And the longer the silence stayed, the more no one felt like they could break it. And the longer no one felt like they could break it, the more everyone wished someone would. Pretty soon it became the kind of silence that made someone invent the word "eerie."

That's when we heard the laughter.

I tried to figure out where it was coming from. It seemed to be coming from everywhere and nowhere at the same time. It was cruel and hard and reminded me of Patrick Docherty frying ants with a magnifying glass.

The whole school was wheeling around on the spot, desperate to get a fix on the noise. Manic laughter is bad enough. Manic laughter that's somehow everywhere but coming from nowhere makes you wonder if you're going completely crazy.

"Over there!" someone shouted, pointing toward the science wing of the school.

We all turned to look. Sure enough, a procession of dark-cloaked figures was coming around the edge of the science wing. Straight toward us.

I shivered.

It wasn't just the weird black academic gowns. It wasn't even the horrible sense of purpose with which they were moving, although that didn't help. It was the way they all marched so completely and utterly in time. I felt like someone had nailed me to the spot.

With fence posts.

As the procession got closer, it got a little less terrifying. The manic laughter stopped, and the gowns began to look less like evil Batman and more like the kind of thing that a certain very old-fashioned principal might wear.

The mystery of the missing teachers was starting to clear up too.

Our homeroom teachers took up their usual positions at the front of the lines, their dusty black gowns billowing behind them. The rest of the teachers faced us, with their backs to the main school building. I waited for Mrs. McKeane to take attendance, but she just stared at a point above my head. She was waiting for something.

Then something happened.

The big blue door that led out from the main building started to open. The teachers in front of the door parted to form two neat lines leading toward the playground. In the doorway stood a man.

Not a tall man, not a wide man, but a man who had figured out how to stand so that a thousand people couldn't take their eyes off him. He stood like a man with a broomstick for a backbone. Like a man who expected to have statues made of him. Like a man born to rule.

If he'd tilted his chin up any higher, he'd have fallen over backward.

As if that wasn't intimidating enough, there was the man's face. The skin on it was blotchy and flushed and covered by sideburns that looked like they needed a zoning permit. The hair on top of his head was a cross between a mane and what you get when you give a two-year-old a crayon. And then there were his eyes.

I don't want to talk about his eyes.

Once he was sure that he had everyone's undivided attention, he started to walk toward us. He took his time. As he passed each teacher, they bowed their heads as a sign of respect. The *thump* of his footsteps was the only sound to be heard on the whole schoolyard. It seemed like even the wind had decided it had better not ruin his entrance.

By the time the man finally took his place in front of Hari, nobody doubted for a second what this all meant.

Victory Piggot wasn't going anywhere.

"Did you really think," he began, "that I was going to slink off with my tail between my legs when I had already come so far? You should've seen their faces!" Victory Piggot indicated the teachers, who didn't even blink. "I gave them a moving speech announcing my retirement, and they pretended to feel sorry for me. We all said how much fun we had and agreed that it'd been an interesting experiment, but that in the long run, it would probably be in everyone's best interests if I was to go quietly on my way. Then they drank to my health. Ha!"

Victory Piggot clenched his bony fists and raised them above his head.

"They did more than just drink *to* my health, they *got* my health!" he boomed. "Isn't it remarkable how far a little bottle can go when it's carefully diluted? There was just enough for all of them to become a little more like me! And as for Mr. Chattersly — well! As you can see, children, he *really* has gotten my health. In fact, he has my teeth! He has my hair! He has *me*!"

The last three words rang through the schoolyard as Victory Piggot wiped the spit triumphantly from his mustache. His chest was heaving, and his eyes shone. He surveyed his minions and waited for a couple of twelfth graders to finish throwing up before delivering his final line.

"Now get out of my sight and get to class!"

The rest of the day was a blur. What was clear was that Hari Patel and Victory Piggot had spun a web of deceit so sticky and dark it could have been made out of molasses.

Hari had known the truth all along. He had known what Victory Piggot planned to do, and he was ready to deal with the fallout.

His first priority was the reporters and how to manage their coverage of the morning's events. So they were invited to the gym for a prearranged press conference. It lasted over an hour. When they came out, the reporters looked dazed, confused, and like none of them had turned down Piggot's offer of as much free wine as they could drink. I heard one of them mumbling something into her phone about Mr. Chattersly being "kept warm and cozy." Another one was singing about goblins.

There was a glimmer of hope when the police turned up. Some of the teachers' families had seen the TV footage and demanded that the police investigate what Piggot had done to their loved ones.

By 3 p.m., the investigation had curled up and died.

There were two big problems. First, and most important, no crime had actually been committed. When the relatives started giving the lead detective a hard time about it, he explained that the last laws to deal with supernatural possession were about four centuries out of date and largely involved drowning witches.

Second, whenever the police tried to interview the teachers to get their story, Victory Piggot made them look stupid. He knew that, on the surface, none of the teachers looked any different. So whenever the police or the teachers themselves tried to draw out Victory Piggot's presence within them, he simply refused to show up.

As a result, Mr. Grieve is now an internet sensation. There's a video of him that's gone viral. He's arguing with himself in the parking lot after the police have just spoken to him. He's shouting at himself and saying that if he doesn't show himself right now, he's going to punch himself so hard he won't know what's hit him. In the end, he tries to run himself over, but can't figure out the logistics.

Thursday, February 7th

This morning, Victory Piggot has dedicated himself to letting us know what a real, old-fashioned education feels like.

It hurts.

I have a sore arm, a bruised rear, and now my brain hurts too. If I have one more fact shoveled into my head, I'm pretty sure the whole thing's going to blow.

Every teacher was the same. We were picked on and shouted at. We sat in rows and repeated what they said about a million times. You weren't allowed to talk, you weren't allowed to fidget, and when Danni Grist tried to use her imagination, all hell broke loose.

For those who survived, there was lunch. I say "lunch." It was a lump of cabbage in a bowl of water. When I'd choked it down, I went up to ask if I could have some dessert.

I won't be doing that again.

The afternoon was the longest school afternoon of my life. Literally. We had Piggot himself for chemistry, and he wasn't going to let anyone go until we could all repeat the entire periodic table back to him perfectly. We got out at 7 p.m. It would have been 6:30 p.m., but Piggot refused to accept that there were any "new" elements discovered in the past hundred and fifty years, and Sally Coyle just couldn't bring herself to leave them out.

Friday, February 8th

Ow.

Saturday, February 9th

Just when I thought I'd learned all there is to know about an old-fashioned education, I found out something new.

It happens on weekends too.

I think my dad was actually trying to hide how funny

he thought it was when he told me the good news. He didn't try very hard.

Nobody else was laughing when I got to school. The Victory Piggot fan club is now officially dead. Instead, the halls were full of hunched shoulders and shuffling feet. As if the whole thing isn't bad enough, Hari's been working on a poster campaign for next week's visit from the Department of Education's Superintendent. Apparently he's interested in "Mr. Piggot's bold new educational initiative." The banner Hari put above the front entrance says NIL SINE LABORE, which roughly translates to "nothing without labor."

The other banners weren't quite so cheerful.

After lunch, for a "treat," the whole school had PE for the rest of the afternoon. I was beginning to wonder if it was Victory Piggot's sick idea of a joke when he charged into the boys' locker room dressed for action.

It wasn't a pretty sight.

His shorts were stained and creased. His cleats looked like something you used to climb Everest with. But there was something far worse than his cleats, his shorts, or even his foul-smelling, multi-striped rugby shirt.

His legs.

It was kind of like leaning over the rail of a really tall building. You didn't want to look down, but you couldn't help yourself.

It was impossible to figure out which part of his leg was which. He may have had knees and ankles, but mounds of curly white hair covered everything. Where you could make out a bit of skin, it was red and angry.

Just like the rest of him.

"Right then, lads! Sports!" he said, much too enthusiastically. "All work and no play makes Jack a dull boy! Eh?" he boomed, slapping Danny Shorey so hard on the back that both his contact lenses came out. "It just started to rain, so I bet you can't wait to start bashing a few bodies and knocking a few heads. Eh? I know I can't."

A room full of vacant faces stared back at him, although Trevor Neave was starting to look interested.

"We'll play a game of mob rugby, and just to make it interesting, we'll have teachers versus students. Hari's volunteered to be referee. First team to get the ball onto the crossbar of the opponents' goal wins. You defend the crossbar closest to the school; we defend the one closest to the railroad tracks. Any questions? No? Good. Let's play."

I don't really know how to play rugby. But it didn't take too long to figure out the rules of *mob* rugby.

There aren't any.

The game started when the ball got flung up high into the air and about one hundred people tried to catch it.

That was the last time I saw it.

The ball disappeared beneath a sea of bodies. I was quite happy to wait for someone to pass it to me.

But when Victory Piggot wasn't trying to get the ball himself, he was walking around the outside of the heap, pushing small kids into it and telling them to stop being such chickens.

Then I got a swift kick up the backside, and the next thing I knew, I was plunged into a whole world of pain.

It was dark. I couldn't breathe. There was a leg pushing against my throat, but I had no idea whose it was. I was getting pinched and bitten, and I think one of the teachers was trying to pull my ear off. I realized I was somewhere in the middle of the heap, but it didn't help. I couldn't figure out which way was up and which way was down, let alone plan an escape. It was like a human avalanche. I'd just figured out that I'd been poking myself in the eye with my elbow when all of a sudden, I realized I could see daylight again. Somebody had managed to get the ball out of the heap and run away, and now the rest of the mob was following.

Harry Johnson went about ten feet before being mown

down by one of Victory Piggot's flying cleats, and another heap soon piled up.

In half an hour, the game had moved about fifteen feet.

Then the rain started really hammering down. Within minutes, the field looked like a battlefield. Every time the heap moved, it took all the grass with it and left behind a muddy, bloody crater. Nobody had the faintest idea who was on which team, and I'm pretty sure we played the last hour without the ball.

When it got so dark you couldn't see anything at all, Victory Piggot blew his whistle.

"Nil-nil!" he boomed, sounding happier than I'd ever heard him. "Excellent game! Everybody back to the locker rooms for a shower."

Those who could walk hobbled back to the locker rooms. Those who couldn't, crawled. Those who couldn't do either just stayed where they'd fallen and hoped no one was going to cut the grass for a few days.

As he jogged past me, I heard Trevor Neave cheerfully ask Victory Piggot how many games of mob rugby ended in nil-nil draws.

Apparently they all do.

When I got home, my mom asked me who I'd gotten into a fight with. She thought I was being sarcastic when I said everyone.

Sunday, February 10th

This morning, the best thing about my life was that it was Sunday.

That lasted until precisely 6:30 a.m., when my dad burst into my room and told me to get changed into my Sunday best because we were going to church. Not content with ruining our school days, Victory Piggot has been telling our parents that he expects them to make sure that "students' home lives are structured, disciplined, and reinforce traditional moral standards."

That's why I look like such an idiot.

It's also why Mom decided to cook a traditional Sunday roast.

It wasn't so much a meal as a massacre. Mom couldn't remember what you were supposed to have with roast beef, so she cooked it in mint sauce, horseradish, and cranberry jelly just to be on the safe side. It was still on fire when Dad wrestled it onto the table. The peas were just about edible, but the roasted potatoes exploded, the carrots boiled dry, and somehow she'd managed to burn the dessert.

It was fruit salad.

If that wasn't bad enough, I was supposed to sit still and

make polite conversation. I'd forgotten just how boring my parents are. After about five minutes, I could feel my eyelids surrendering. The next thing I knew, my head hit the table, and I got sent to my room for my appalling table manners.

Just great.

Monday, February 11th

Last night, I fell asleep as soon as I'd finished writing in my journal. I'd been planning to spend the rest of the evening trying to figure out what to do about Victory Piggot, but it's hard to come up with a cunning plan when you're so tired that you can't remember how to brush your own teeth.

School started with the longest assembly ever. There were rules, there was singing, there were more rules, there was sitting, there was standing, there was much, much more singing, and there was asking for forgiveness for what wicked and terrible children we all are.

Just when I thought it couldn't get any worse, the state superintendent decided to join in.

At first I thought he had something wrong with his eyes. He was peering around the auditorium like he was trying to see his audience. I was wondering how he hadn't noticed the hundreds of bored kids in front of him when I realized he wasn't looking for us at all. He was checking out where the TV cameras were. When he found one, he made sure he smiled right at it.

"I must say, children," he said to the camera, "how refreshing it is to see a school assembly that isn't accompanied by the constant shuffling of feet and chewing of gum. And I hope you appreciate how much better you present yourselves because of it."

The superintendent spotted another camera on the other side of the auditorium and gave it his and-now-I'm-going-to-be-serious face.

"Of course, there's more to school than good behavior and discipline, but I believe that a return to these traditional values is well overdue. Modern society would benefit a great deal from people like you having more structure to your lives and a greater respect for your elders."

The superintendent swung back to the original camera. If he'd bothered to look, he would have noticed that he'd completely lost his actual audience. Not in the sense that they couldn't follow what he was saying, but because most kids were still trying to figure out who he was speaking to.

"I'm going to be around your school all day," he continued, in a tone that made it sound like a good thing. "And I hope to see more of the excellent behavior that has attracted me here in the first place. As you may have heard, we are considering making this a flagship school, a school which all others will aspire to. It'll also mean plenty of money for Mr. Piggot and the ambitious plans he has for you.

"However, I don't want to keep you any longer. And so, with your permission, Principal . . ." The superintendent looked at Piggot, who smiled indulgently and gave him a nod. "Class dismissed! I've always wanted to say that."

Mom and Dad forced me to watch the news when I got home.

"Look! You're on TV," Mom said excitedly when the camera showed a close-up of the school's main entrance.

That was about as much of the school as I recognized.

The rest of the news report was filmed in one of the computer science rooms. It's been restricted for the past few days. Now I know why. Someone has filled it with fancy pictures and student project posters where everything is spelled correctly, and Hari was there, having a "chat" with the superintendent about how much fun computer programming could be and how Mr. Piggot had turned around a "failing culture of student-centered learning" at the school.

Even Mom started to get a little suspicious.

"I don't think we've met that new teacher, have we?" she asked as a random pretty woman had a close-up taken of her.

"Neither has anyone else," I told her. "She's an actress."

"Your school's kind of funny sometimes, isn't it?" she said thoughtfully. "Of course, as long as you're happy there . . ."

"Me? I'm ecstatic! Who wouldn't want two completely psychotic principals in two semesters?"

"Well, that's good, then," she said, taking the dinner plates into the kitchen and once again demonstrating that she couldn't detect sarcasm if it looked her in the face and told her she didn't look a day over twenty-one.

  Tuesday, February 12th

I couldn't get to sleep last night. The house was still, but my mind was all over the place.

Every time I shut my eyes, visions of Hari, Piggot, and

the superintendent
kept swimming into
my head and making
faces at me. The final
straw was Victory
Piggot grinning madly
as he put a giant
match to *TWW*.

That did it.

No one burns my
baby.

I got up and pulled out
my laptop. There was
no time for an actual paper, but I'd just thought of the
next best thing. The floating faces had given me an idea.

A couple of weeks ago, Mr. Storey had been trying
to teach us something in computer science. I can't
remember what it was, because I was way more
interested in watching how he reset the startup page for
the whole school network while he thought no one was
looking. I had a feeling it would come in handy.

So, for the past few days, everybody has been logging on to school computers to find this "motivational" message all over their screens:

> The Child Who Toils Will Never Spoil

This morning they booted up to something a little different.

BREAKING NEWS FROM
THE WOODFORD WORD!

SUPERINTENDENT
IS A SUPER IDIOT

State Department of Education Superintendent Michael Morrissey took his eye off the ball yesterday in announcing that Woodford School and its mad master, Victory Piggot, should become a "flagship school."

My grade was sent to the gym after second period. I thought maybe we were going there for another assembly, but it was worse than that.

We were going there for gym.

Victory Piggot stood in the middle of the basketball court, Hari at his side. They were surrounded by wall bars, weights, and those weird boxes you're supposed to jump over.

"Good morning, sixth graders," he said, clearly replacing the words "sixth graders" with "scum of the earth" in his head as he did. "It seems we're left with you. Improbable as it may sound, one of you must be the elusive Jonny Jakes, Fiona Friend, or whoever it was who vandalized our electronic computer system this morning.

"So, before we all get started, would anyone care to step forward and save their fellow classmates from —" Piggot and Hari caught each other's eyes and smiled "— a rather *vigorous* workout? Any volunteers? No?" Piggot sneered. "Good. We'll carry on then, shall we?"

At that point, a few of the more naturally sadistic teachers came in to join us. They were all wearing shorts and, like Hari, had stopwatches and whistles hanging around their necks. For some reason, they were also carrying mops and buckets.

I didn't take it as a good sign.

"Look around you," Victory Piggot continued once they were all in. "There are thirty exercise stations around the gymnasium. In a moment, you will go to one of them, where you will start that particular exercise. You will be under the close supervision of my colleagues, who will encourage you to do the best you can."

As he said the word "encourage," several teachers cracked their knuckles. Victory Piggot waited for the echo to die down.

"After one minute, I will blow my whistle and then you will move on to the next station and so on. Any questions?"

Some idiot decided to put his hand up.

"Yes?" Victory Piggot asked.

"Um, when do we stop, sir?" the idiot asked.

Victory Piggot smiled. He walked over to the idiot and bent down. He gently took hold of the idiot's ear and spoke just loudly enough for the rest of us to hear.

"You haven't quite got the hang of this yet, have you?" he began sweetly. Then his voice began to rise dramatically. "You start when I tell you to start. You breathe when I tell you to breathe! And you stop when I tell you to stop, which will be when I've found out who Jonny Jakes is! Now get over there and get ready to climb up that rope!"

Piggot blew his whistle in the poor idiot's ear. Within seconds, the rest of the room divided itself up. The torture was about to begin.

I remember seeing a film about an old war in history class once. There were soldiers trying to run across muddy fields full of barbed wire, and there were giant explosions going off all around them. The teacher had asked us to try to imagine what it must have been like. It was difficult at the time.

Now I have an idea.

Within minutes, the gym was full of pain. I started off doing push-ups. I'd done twenty when I was "encouraged" to stop just pushing my butt up and down and keep my body straight.

It stung.

I did five proper push-ups before the whistle blew and I was "encouraged" to climb up and down the wall bars. They were already really sweaty, and I slipped and smacked my chin on one.

"Stop bleeding!" Victory Piggot screeched as I wobbled past him on my way to the rope climb.

It didn't go well.

I can't remember much about the other stations. It was all kind of a blur. There was running involved and jumping and something called a medicine ball that didn't make me feel any better and lots and lots of "encouragement." After every minute, Piggot would ask for a confession, but I was determined not to give up.

At one point,
I remember
wondering if Norris
was going to crack
under the pressure.
I looked around
for him and saw
him giving Freddy
Harris a piggyback
ride between some
cones while Mr.
King threw tennis
balls at him.

He looked like he was enjoying himself.

One agonizing hour later, Piggot blew his whistle for
the last time. Maybe he thought that Jonny Jakes was
just too much of a hero to give up, or maybe he'd just
had enough of the smell. I let out a sigh of relief and
collapsed in a heap.

It was a popular choice.

Norris and I were heading outside for lunch when a whispered voice from behind the recycling bins told me that perhaps the day's torture wasn't yet over.

It was Julie Singh.

"Over here," she hissed. "We need to talk."

"There is no 'we,'" I protested. "There stopped being a 'we' the moment you wrote for *him*."

"I'm sorry," she hissed, still behind the bins. "Feel better?"

"Yes," I admitted. I crouched down until I could make out her face. She was wedged tight behind the paper bin, and I could see she'd been crying. "What is it?"

"We have to do something."

"About what?"

"What do you think?" Julie stifled a sob. "About him! And will you just get back here so I don't have to look quite so pathetic!"

"Okay, which particular him?" I asked, once I'd squeezed behind the bin next to Julie.

"Both of them. Piggot's bad enough, but now Hari's become a monster too."

"He won't take no for an answer," another familiar voice piped up from behind the glass recycling bin. "He's forcing us to be part of his propaganda machine," Sally moaned.

"What's a propaganda machine?" Norris wanted to know as he squeezed in next to me.

"He wants us to write anything he tells us to," Julie explained.

"Or what?" I asked.

"Or we're the first." Sally's voice was thin and shaky. She looked terrified.

"The first what?" Norris said.

"The first to be t-tested," Sally stammered. "Mr. Piggot wants to start his old experiments up again. If we don't do what Hari asks, we're going to be the first guinea pigs."

"So what are you going to do?" I wanted to know.

"I don't know!" Julie snapped. "That's why I'm asking for your help behind a recycling bin! I said I'm sorry, what more do you . . ."

Suddenly the bin me and Norris were crouched behind was wheeled away. In its place appeared Victory Piggot and his right-hand man.

"These two?" Hari asked Piggot in a disdainful tone, pointing at us. "Are you sure they're what you're after, sir? They're fairly pathetic specimens."

"I'm sure," Piggot growled. "They were in Chattersly's office the day I arrived. They were never properly punished then, so I see no reason for them not to give something back to the school now."

"As you wish, sir. These two," Hari commanded. The two lab technicians who had rolled the bin away came forward, grabbed us by the elbows, and marched us into the school building. Hari and Piggot fell in behind us.

I looked over my shoulder. Julie was clutching her mouth in shock. For a split second, I wondered if we'd just been set up, but then I remembered that she couldn't act to save her life. It was one of her more attractive personality traits.

As we were led across the playground, no one looked remotely surprised to see a couple of sixth graders being dragged around by Piggot's lackeys. I had the tech with the purple hair. Her nails were digging into my skin.

"That hurts," I told her. "You don't have to pinch me!"

Piggot whacked the back of my head.

"Keep a civil tongue in your head, boy."

"But . . . w-where are you taking us?" I spluttered. Stars swam in front of my eyes and fear cartwheeled around my guts as the prospect of Piggot's experiments suddenly took an unwanted grip on my imagination. "You can't just . . ."

This time it was Hari who cuffed the other side of my head.

"Mr. Piggot can do whatever he sees fit in order to maintain order at the school," he said.

More stars started to dance in front of me. The grip on my elbow tightened as we headed for the stairs. I had a horrible feeling I knew where we were going.

Sure enough, we soon found ourselves in the gloomy hallway leading to Piggot's old office. He had fitted it out with some old-fashioned lamps, but it was still cold and full of shadows.

It suited him.

I was surprised when we halted. Instead of Piggot's old office, we had stopped outside another door. It was protected with three different padlocks.

"Inside," Piggot instructed us once Hari had undone the locks.

"No," said Norris. It was a brave move.

But foolish.

The lab tech with the tattoos struck him a harsh blow to the kidneys, and he was dragged, groaning, into a leather chair and strapped down.

I got shoved into one next to him.

We were in what was unmistakably a laboratory. There were test tubes, Bunsen burners, clamps, and frothing bottles of liquid. Among other things, I was starting to seriously regret not going to the bathroom earlier.

"Now then, boys, there's no need to be alarmed," Piggot began, in a softer voice than usual. "We're not going to particularly harm you."

It was the least reassuring thing anyone has ever said to me.

"I just need to ensure that the breakthrough research I began is not lost," Piggot continued. The anger in his face had gone. It was a shame it had to be replaced by the crazy stare of a mad scientist. "You understand, don't you?"

I could tell it was a rhetorical question by the way the lab techs were putting gags in our mouths.

"Don't worry about those," Piggot said. "They're just for your protection — to stop you from biting your tongues off. Ready?"

"Ready, sir," Hari said. He was staring at me. Weirdly. It was like he'd just seen me properly for the first time. "But can I just ask this boy a few questions?"

"Another time, Hari!" Piggot snapped. "Science first. Questions later. Now, who shall we begin with?"

My arms were firmly strapped down, so I jerked my head in Norris's direction. Unfortunately, Piggot mistook it for a nod.

"Good lad!" he boomed. "Take one for the team, eh? Now then, this won't hurt too much."

I closed my eyes. It wasn't like I needed to actually see the gigantic needle heading toward me. I felt a sharp sting in the top of my left arm, followed by a strong, dull ache.

"That's it. Not too bad, was it?" Piggot said, bizarrely

cheerful. "Sit tight while we do your friend. Then one more little stab, and we'll be done."

I kept my eyes shut and tried not to imagine what Piggot was up to. He hadn't done an experiment in over a century. Just because he wasn't trying to deliberately hurt us didn't mean he wasn't accidentally going to kill us.

A second jab went into my left arm. It was sore already, and I yelled in pain. I could feel the warm ooze of something being pumped in. I felt faint. My head was on fire and everything was spinning. Before I knew it, I'd puked all over my lap.

"UUUGH!" Hari yelled. He'd been in the firing line and was covered in globules of vomit. Piggot wasn't too pleased, either.

"Subject one unsuitable!" he shouted at the lab technicians. He tugged his mustache and creased his forehead. "Unable to retain active ingredient."

One lab tech took a note. The second injected Norris. Piggot watched nervously. A minute and no puking later, he cheered up again.

"Subject two suitable!" he crowed. "Detain him for observation for ninety minutes." He smiled and patted Norris on the shoulder as if he were a pet. Then his expression darkened as he made his way back to my chair.

"Your friend, however, is going to leave us. This, of course, is with the understanding that if he mentions what has happened here to anyone, and I mean anyone!" He glared at me. Hari hadn't stopped glaring at me. "Then I will dedicate the rest of my time on this earth to finding a particularly unpleasant active ingredient that he can digest. *Permanently.*"

"Sir, before he goes, could I just . . ."

"Not now, Hari," Piggot interrupted angrily. "I want this . . . inferior specimen out of my way. Immediately. I am not interested in failure."

I tried to stare Piggot down to show I hadn't taken his insults personally, but his eyes were bulging with manic energy, so I gave up. Behind him, Norris was angrier than I'd ever seen him. His wrists were straining against the leather straps and a vein in his neck was pulsing dangerously. He was giving Piggot the kind of stare that made anyone who wanted to tackle him on the football field suddenly realize their shoelaces were undone.

On Piggot's signal, the lab techs undid my straps. Hari was literally biting his lip in order to avoid upsetting his master further. I racked my brains trying to figure out why he'd started to suspect me. Had he seen me in the hall back when we'd found the diary? Had I done my English homework too well again and blown him away with my literary genius?

As I got up, I tried to give Norris a sign that I wouldn't rest until I'd defeated the forces of darkness.

It was a shame it sprayed some of my puke on him.

I stumbled up to the main hallway. Images of Norris, strapped down and struggling, were racing around my head. The remaining contents of my stomach weren't exactly playing it cool, either. I held on to a doorway for support.

I made it to the bathroom, pulled my sweater off, and threw it straight in the trash. Then I splashed some water on my face and began to feel a little more human. I checked myself in the mirror, looking into my eyes for answers.

Did I still have what it took to defeat the forces of darkness?

Tick.

Even when they stuck big needles into people?

There was a longer pause.

Tick.

Relieved, I headed out again. I guess I was going home, but I couldn't be sure. My brain had decided to let my feet make their own decisions while it tried to figure out how to free Norris from Piggot's clutches.

I got as far as the next corner before a pair of hands grabbed me and pulled me into the Drop-In Zone. The same hands pushed me onto the bean bags.

"I wonder how much they'd give me?" Michelle Bell's face leered over me. "What do you think you're worth?"

I tried to collect my thoughts. It wasn't easy with the room spinning around so quickly.

"Uh, what?"

"You. Loser. I bet you could make me a lot richer."

"Uh, what?" I wondered again. I was struggling to access the rest of my vocabulary.

"Although I guess I'd have to prove it somehow." Michelle said, grinning. She put her hands on her hips. "I mean, you're not much to look at, are you? That's why it took me so long!"

She reached into her pocket. It was her turn to show me some pictures.

"Of course, I could use the picture I took of you raiding Mr. Chattersly's competition box. Or perhaps the sneaky snapshot I took of you filling the lockers with *The Woodford Word* last week."

I tried to think of something to save me, but nothing came. On top of everything else, Michelle Bell had beaten me at my own game. She bent down to grab my wrists.

"Easy, nerd!" she said as I lashed out. "I'm pulling you up, not taking you prisoner."

"What?"

Michelle laughed. "It's your lucky day, *Jonny*. I've decided you're worth more on the loose than you are in whatever dungeon Piggot's got lined up for you. I just saw Hari — he was running up from the basement calling your name. Your real name. It's pretty lucky everyone else has gone home. I think he's starting to figure out your identity too."

"But how . . ."

"Put him down!"

Michelle Bell let go of my hand and turned to see Julie and Sally advancing cautiously toward her. She assessed the situation.

"Or what? You're going to hit me with rolls of art paper?"

Julie tried not to look embarrassed. "If we have to!"

"OMG!" Michelle squawked suddenly. "It's *all* of you, isn't it? *The Woodford Word*. Losers united!" While she was distracted, I reached down to see if my fingers could find something better for an improvised weapon.

They didn't.

"Jonny, if anything, a bean bag is even less terrifying. All right! Enough!" Michelle's smile vanished as we continued to threaten her with stationery and soft furnishings. "I'm not here to rat you out, Jonny. I'm here —" she sighed "— to save you."

Sally and Julie halted their advance. "Oh," Sally said, confused. "That's what *we* were doing."

"Well, give me a hand, then. Hari's suspicious," Michelle explained again. "Him and that lab tech with the weird hair are running around looking for you."

"So we need to get you out of here," Julie summarized. "What about Norris?"

I shook my head. "Piggot said he'd let him go in a little while. He's still down there."

"You don't look so good," Sally noted. "Can I get you anything?"

"No time," Julie cut in, looking out the window. "The lab tech's heading this way. We need a disguise."

We looked around. The Drop-In Zone was big on cushions, but it didn't have much to offer on the disguise front. Unfortunately, Michelle Bell then realized she had a makeup bag.

"No way!" I protested as she shook it at me.

"You don't have a choice," Michelle said, pulling out a metal tube and revealing a hideous pink lipstick.

"And we're going to have to be quick!" Julie commanded.

The girls stared at me. I stared right back. If I was going to become a girl, they'd have to make me.

It turns out Michelle Bell is very good at that kind of thing.

Three minutes later, I was ready. We didn't get far.

"Where are you going?" the tattooed lab tech demanded.

"Home," Michelle replied, gripping my arm to prevent me from wiping off my eyeshadow.

"Have you seen a boy?"

We shook our heads.

"What's with all the makeup?" the lab tech wanted to know, pulling her face close to mine. I looked down and fiddled with my skirt.

I hope to never repeat that sentence again.

"She's just been dumped," Michelle replied for me. "She doesn't want her boyfriend to know she's been crying." The lab tech kept her face inches from mine, examining my "boyfriend" misery. Satisfied, she let out a harsh laugh.

"Welcome to the real world!" she jeered. Then she lost interest and headed back down the hall. We ran off in the other direction.

I hoped it would have a huge, gaping hole in the ground.

"Thanks," I gasped when we'd made it off the school grounds. I wiped my forehead. My hand instantly became covered in makeup. "I think."

"Any time," Michelle said with a grin. "Maybe next time you can be a blonde?"

Sally tried not to laugh. Julie was less successful.

"Okay, so I'm going to go home now, and you guys are going to do all that saving-the-day-in-secret stuff. Just remember, you can call me if you need me," Michelle continued, starting to head off. "Later, losers."

I wasn't sure what to say, so I waved. The girls joined in.

"Right," I said when she'd gone. "Priority one: shower. Priority two: meet you at Norris's house later."

"If he gets out," Sally said, worried.

"Oh, I saw the look on his face when I left," I assured her. "Trust me. He's getting out."

Once we'd gone our separate ways, I ran all the way home. Unnatural, but it had its advantages. I got home before my parents and was seen by as few people as possible.

As I burst through the door, the phone rang.

"Yeah?" I panted, out of breath. There was a pause. I could feel confusion on the other end of the line.

"Hello, could I speak to your mom or dad, please?"

The sweat froze on my forehead.

It was Hari.

He was trying to do a fake voice, but I'd have recognized it anywhere. I calculated swiftly: he'd paused because he'd been unsure; the panting had masked my voice; he'd asked for my parents to be on the safe side; I was better than Hari at fake voices.

"That would be difficult!" I blustered, doing my best to sound like my dad as I deliberately kept up the panting. "Seeing as they live in Florida. Look, who is it and what is it? I just got back from my run, and I need a shower."

Hari bought it, but all I'd bought was a little time. He said I needed to bring my son in for an urgent meeting with the principal, and I agreed. But when I didn't get marched down to school within half an hour, Hari was going to know he'd been tricked. It was time to disappear.

Priority one was going to have to wait.

Ten minutes later, I was crawling through Norris's bedroom window and flopping onto his floor. I'd left a note on my bedroom door explaining to my parents that I was running away, but for them not to feel bad, because it wasn't their fault. Just to buy more time, I "accidentally" left the train times to Cape Cod scribbled on a note on my nightstand.

A muffled voice came from the region of the bed. To my relief, Norris had made it home.

"Go away. I'm not hungry."

"Norris," I whispered. "It's me. What happened?"

The covers rustled. Norris poked his face out.

"I don't know how you live like this," Norris replied gloomily. "Hey, why do you look like a girl?"

"Live like what?" I asked, eager to steer the conversation back to the original question.

"With this," he said, pointing to his stomach.

"Huh?"

"With this," he said, pointing to his stomach again. "It doesn't do anything!"

"I'm not getting what 'this' is," I explained. "What did Piggot inject you with? Did he pass on something from me?"

"He gave me your appetite," Norris groaned. "He probably tried to give you mine. You know, like the wren and the spider in Jennings's diary? It's terrible. How can someone only like three types of food?"

"What other types are there?"

Norris groaned again.

"Hari knows my secret identity," I told him, hoping the news would snap him out of it. "He thinks my dad is about to bring me into school. It's a nightmare. I can't go to school, I can't go home, I . . ."

"Slow down," Norris complained. "Think it through. And maybe take a shower while you do it," he added, wrinkling his nose.

Norris helped me sneak into the bathroom. I was a lot happier with my appearance when I came out. Norris was much happier with the aroma. I was also surprisingly pleased to see the girls at Norris's window.

"Norris!" Julie said with a sigh of relief as she slithered in. Sally followed behind. She looked ashamed.

"Did it hurt?"

"A little," Norris replied, patting his stomach awkwardly. "It could've been worse."

"It should have been me," Julie said apologetically.

"And me," Sally agreed.

"Uh, no," I interrupted. "Technically, I think you'll find no one should've been getting experimented on! Now, maybe we should stop feeling sorry for ourselves and figure out what we're going to do about it!" I punched the bed for emphasis. "We need to get back into that lab."

"No!" Norris protested.

"Why?" asked Sally.

"Proof." Julie took the word from my mouth. Then she added some more of her own. "Documents, pictures of what he's up to. Plus we have to stop what he's doing. He's managed to change Norris's appetite — what's he going to do next?"

"I am not being turned into anything else!" I said with feeling.

"I just had a horrible thought," Sally muttered. I could see that she was trying to keep control of the contents of her stomach.

"What is it?" I asked.

"What if he wants everyone to turn into him?" Sally replied, her voice hushed.

"It's already happening," Norris agreed after a heavy silence. "Haven't you noticed the teachers? He's not just in their heads anymore. He's spreading."

I nodded. Norris was right. It was subtle, but it was there in the little things. The teachers were marching more than they were walking, their hands were gradually tightening into fists, and their voices were becoming deeper.

Julie had seen it too. She nodded. "Then we have to act tonight."

"And do what?" Sally wanted to know.

"The laboratory," Julie answered. "We have to stop Piggot's work. Destroy it. In fact, what are we waiting for? Let's go right now!"

I held up my hand. "Too soon. They'll be expecting something."

"And they'll be awake," Norris agreed. We caught each other's eye. We both knew where we were going next with this. At our last sleepover, we'd been looking at a website about the world's secret police. It had some handy tips.

"Four a.m.," I began.

"Universally recognized and proven to be the best time for a raid," Norris continued, quoting from *Ultimate Soldier*.

"Targets are fatigued."

"They lose control of higher functions."

"And are psychologically compromised in seventy-eight percent of all . . ."

"Enough of the boy talk," Julie snapped. "I get it. What are we going to do until then?"

Norris tapped his nose and caught my eye again. "Use the Ultimate Soldier's best secret weapon."

Julie sighed. "Which is?"

"Sleep," we said together smugly.

And to think my mom believes that the internet rots your brain.

4 a.m. February 13th. Masked figures break in to a secret underground laboratory. Their mission: to save mankind.

Again.

I am *so* getting a movie made of my life.

Julie had already pocketed her mom's school keys, so the main entrance was no problem. My lock-picking kit made short work of the padlocks on the lab door.

A science laboratory is a home away from home for Sally, so she quickly put us to work. She told me and Norris what to photograph while she and Julie raided the filing cabinets.

"So now we destroy it?" I asked when we had gathered the proof we needed.

Sally shrugged. "I guess." You could tell that the idea of undoing years of groundbreaking research wasn't going down easily.

"Sounds good to me!" Norris said with considerably more enthusiasm. He grabbed a bottle with *mercaptoacetic acid* on the label. "I think I'm finally getting my appetite back, and I'm *not* going through that again."

"Watch out!" Sally warned as Norris raised his arm to smash the bottle on the floor.

It was too late.

A vile smell exploded out of the broken bottle. About three seconds later, the contents of our stomachs exploded into the sinks.

"Better out than in," Norris consoled us once we could all breathe again. "I guess I didn't have anything left to be sick with."

"What was *that*?" Julie wanted to know, tears streaming from her eyes.

"It's a volatile compound rich in sulfur," Sally explained with her hand still hovering by her mouth.

"It stinks!" I complained, wiping my mouth. Then I stopped mid-wipe.

My stomach was still cramping and my head was swimming, but an idea was trying to say hello from deep inside my brain. I held a finger to my lips for silence.

"What is it?" Julie whispered, her thoughts immediately turning to the door and the hallway beyond.

"Shhh," I insisted. "I'm trying to think. Somebody said something. Us. Just now. I think it's important. Sally, what did you just say?"

"Uh . . . it's a volatile compound."

"It wasn't that. Julie?"

"What was that?"

"Nope. Norris?"

Norris puffed out his cheeks in the effort to remember. "You were puking," he thought aloud. "What do you say when someone's puking?"

"Yuck?" I guessed.

Norris shook his head. "It was something else."

Sally shut her eyes and tried to replay the conversation in her head. "Better out than in," she said triumphantly a few moments later.

"And he said he had nothing left in his stomach because of his appetite," Julie added.

At last my thought made its way to the surface.

"That's it! All this —" I indicated the camera, the documents we'd stolen, and the broken glass on the floor. "That doesn't put an end to it. It's in here," I tapped my head. "In Piggot's head. He'll figure it out again. It's *him* we need to get rid of."

"But what about the teachers?" Julie asked. "He's infected all of them. Do we have to get rid of them as well?"

"It's a nice idea," I agreed. "But it's only what's *in* them that's the problem. We don't have to get rid of the teachers, as long as we can get Piggot out of them."

"And how do we do that?" Julie wanted to know.

I looked around the lab, at all the mysterious potions left on the shelves. I visualized and then I grinned.

"By making science a whole lot more fun."

We crept into Norris's garage at 5:30 a.m. and gently dumped our backpacks before turning on the light. We'd taken what we needed from the lab and went on a quick shopping trip for a few essential items.

Norris peered cautiously outside as the rest of us took in the hulks of dismantled engines spread out around us. Tools lined the walls and two steel carts were crammed full of more. It looked like Norris's dad knew his way around a wrench.

"We're okay," Norris assured us as he came back in. "No lights in the house, and the street is empty."

"First things first, then," Sally instructed. "Everyone grab a mask."

We pulled on the masks and got to work. Norris was in charge of engineering. Sally did the chemistry. Me and Julie did what we were told.

An hour of dangerous and foul-smelling work later, we were ready for the next phase.

Norris and I pulled on the backpacks again and headed off to school. Julie and Sally went to organize backup and make an appearance at breakfast.

I made it, undetected, to assembly. Or, as Victory Piggot has decided to rename it, Whole School Singing Practice. Apparently it was going to be an experience that united us in our "core values" while providing "hearty exercise" and "joyous fellowship."

I can confidently report that the students had a different way of describing it.

The "joyous fellowship" part definitely looked in short supply as everyone squeezed into the stuffy auditorium, although you could argue that there was some "hearty exercise" between the tough kids and anyone else who tried to sit near them.

When the students were seated, the teachers handed out dusty old hymn books before taking their places on the stage above in comfy chairs.

Presumably the teachers' "core values" translated into sitting as far away from the kids as possible.

"Hymn five hundred and sixty-one: 'Rise from your graves, ye dead,'" Piggot commanded, forcing everyone back to their feet again. "But, before we begin, I am sure you are aware that there are a couple of school matters we need to address."

Piggot stalked to the front of the stage. His eyebrows lowered and his eyes glinted below them like diamonds stuck in a thorn bush.

"On the plus side," he began, in a voice that could trigger avalanches, "the superintendent has decided to make our school a flagship school! That means that what goes on at Woodford School will provide a basis for improvement for the rest of the country!

"Just think," he said, pounding the lectern, "soon the whole United States of America will once again be back on the path to greatness! Punishment will pave the way and discipline will no longer be a dirty word!

"However!" he shrieked, hitting the top of his crescendo. "First there is the matter of our snake in the grass. Our toad in the hole. The one who wants to ruin it for everyone: Jonny Jakes."

I looked across at Norris. He wondered if that should be our signal. I shook my head.

"And now," Piggot continued, "thanks to Hari, we are going to flush the viper from its nest."

Norris looked again. I shook my head again. I wanted to know what animal I was going to be next.

And besides, timing was everything.

"That's right," Hari piped up. "Boys and girls. Fellow students. I am sure that you, like me, have often wondered who Jonny Jakes really is. Well, yesterday, I finally figured it out."

Hari soaked up the attention of the auditorium and spun out his moment of triumph.

"And today, now, we will put an end to his campaign of fear and mistruth. In a few seconds, with the press of a button, his face will appear on this projector screen. Just before I do that, however, we want you to know two things. The first is that the reward for handing Jonny Jakes over to us is five hundred dollars."

A murmuring filled the room.

A slightly more enthusiastic murmuring than I would have liked.

Norris looked across again. I nodded and held my hand up, ready to count down from five on my fingers.

Julie, Sally, and Michelle began to move stealthily toward their positions.

Five.

Hari carried on, oblivious to the two heavily armed figures hanging among the lighting bars and scenery above him. "The second thing you need to know is that no one . . ."

Four.

" . . . is leaving here until he is brought to us . . ."

Three.

". . . or we are told exactly where we can find him."

Two.

"Good." Hari appreciated the stony silence. "I'm glad that's understood."

One.

"So, let's do this."

Zero.

My hand became a fist. It was showtime.

Hari went for the remote control, but before he got there, he was plunged into darkness. Julie had killed the lights above the stage, and at the same instant, Sally had rattled the red curtain across the front of it.

A second later, six pairs of rubber gloves full of butyric acid sank softly through the darkness toward the bewildered teachers below. I could hear the squelch as the gloves hit the floor. I was glad I had a mask on to protect me from what happened next.

Sally was right. If you want to make people sick, then a very good place to start is with the smell of barf.

The rotten eggs we'd gotten from the trash went next in four more rubber gloves. This time, even my mask couldn't completely block out the smell. It had been a touch of genius to mix the rotten eggs with the milk.

Especially when you think of just how out of date it was.

Happy that we had gotten things successfully under way, me and Norris switched on our headlamps. I was treated to a spectacular aerial view of Mr. Chang. He was clutching his throat and stumbling around in his own vomit.

Looking around, it seemed to be a standard maneuver.

We rappeled down. One hand controlled the descender, and the other one got busy on the trigger of the spray bottles we'd unhooked from our utility belts. It was time for trimethylamine to join the party. You could tell Sally had formulated it perfectly by the way the varnish on the stage's wooden floor started peeling.

With our feet dangling above the heads of the stricken teachers, me and Norris stopped our descents and swung the straps around on our backs. Taking care to fire away from each other, we put Norris's improvised puke pumps to work. The putrescine cocktail shot out.

So did more vomit.

When we finally hit the stage and unclipped, a few teachers tried to come after us. In the crisscross of the beams of our headlamps, it was kind of like a zombie movie where they all start to close in on you. Really slowly. One of teachers, with his hand over his mouth, got a hold of my mask, but just as he was about to try to pull it off, Norris managed to uncork something very unpleasant right under his nose. All of a sudden, my attacker had other matters that needed his attention.

It's amazing how fast people can think when they're desperate. Another teacher had put a cushion cover over his head to protect himself from the stench. It was working well enough for him to be making steady progress toward where he thought the fire exit was.

I reached down for the glass vial tucked in my sock and thrust it up under the cushion cover. Then I crushed it in my gloved hand. A warm, purplish ooze trickled over my wrist. Followed by a green torrent of stomach juice.

The teacher sank to his knees.

It felt cruel to keep going, but the plan was only going to work if we did it right. "Better out than in" meant we couldn't leave anything behind. If we'd learned anything about Victory Piggot, it was that he wasn't leaving unless he absolutely had to.

Somewhere in the background, I could hear that the student evacuation process on the other side of the curtains was in its final stages. It was a good thing too. The curtains were starting to curl up and die, just like everyone else wanted to do behind them.

Eventually our supplies were exhausted, and I was as eager as the teachers to get out of there. The rubber on the mask was starting to give up, and the hideous stink was trying to creep in. We waited as long as we could as teacher after teacher heaved and retched until nothing more seemed to be coming out. Then I stuck my hand through the curtains and waved.

The lights above the stage came back on, and the three masked girls ran in to join us. We gave each other the thumbs-up.

Each of the girls was carrying two large funnel-shaped devices strapped to their back. They looked like cosmic ray guns, but they were better than that.

They were blow-dryers.

Big blow-dryers.

A tidal wave of hot air began to roll around the stage.

A few seconds later, a foul mist of vomit vapor started to drift up from the floor. Soon the mist had become a fog, and I couldn't see a thing. I kept wiping the visor on my mask, but it didn't help.

I was getting panicky with the smell and the heat and the sense that something was wrong. It felt like I was going to suffocate. Climbing over the moaning bodies, I eventually made it to the fire exit and shoved it open. The fog wobbled and then decided it needed some air.

It wasn't the only one.

In a few seconds, there was a full-on gale as fresh air flooded in and the fog flew out.

The stage was full of pale-faced teachers clutching their stomachs and begging for water. We couldn't risk it, though. Who knew, maybe somewhere in the mist, the faintest trace of Victory Piggot was still alive and all it needed was one contaminated drink and we'd be back where we started.

I pointed at the door and mimed crawling outside. The grown-ups got the message. Soon there was a long line of teachers crawling toward the playground. Their tongues were hanging out and their eyeballs were bursting.

I couldn't resist taking a picture.

Out in the open, a few of the teachers felt up to asking questions. "What's going on?" was pretty popular, followed by "Why do I smell so much?," "Why do I have corn in my hair?," and finally, "Is he gone?"

I spun around. The nagging sense of something being wrong had just turned into a big, fat reality.

"Where's Piggot?" I yelled at the others. "Or Chattersly?"

Michelle Bell pulled her mask off for a better view.

"Not here," she said, shaking her head.

"When did you last see him?" Julie asked.

"And what about Hari?" Sally wondered.

"Nooo!" I stamped the ground in frustration.

"Owww!" Ms. Frustup yelped. I'd just stepped on her outstretched finger. "That way," she said hoarsely. "Both of them. Wrapped up in Piggot's gown."

"Where do you think he's taking him?" Sally asked as we ran off in the direction of Ms. Frustup's crumpled finger.

"The lab," I panted. "It has to be. Come on!"

"Wait," Michelle Bell demanded. "There's no point going in the main door."

"I can pick the locks," I pointed out.

"He'll be ready for you, though. I know another way."

Instead of the main building, Michelle led us out to the playground. Specifically, the part of it behind the recycling bins, where we'd met Julie and Sally the day before.

"Look. Here." Michelle pointed to an iron grille set into the concrete. Then she lay down on her stomach and put her ear to it. "Listen."

We fanned out around the grille on our stomachs, our ears close to the bars.

"There, there," a voice drifted up to us. It was Piggot's, but even weirder than normal. It sounded as if he was trying to comfort a baby. *"Just think about what we can do, Hari. Together. Forever."*

I felt dizzy. The pages of Robert Jennings's diary were suddenly swimming in front of my eyes.

"Haven't I done enough, sir?" a second voice floated up. It was terrified, just like another schoolboy had been over a hundred years ago.

"You have served me well, Hari," Piggot explained patiently. *"And soon you shall serve me further. Forever! And then Hari, then the world is ours."*

"Switch your lamps on," Michelle whispered. "See. There's a door, down there. I bet he doesn't even know it's there."

We peered through the grate in the light of our headlamps. Sure enough, there was an old door with a small vent at the top through which we'd heard the voices.

"Probably had steps down to it years ago," Michelle explained. "They've walled them up, though. Give me a hand, Norris."

"Do you have your stuff for the lock?" Julie asked as Norris and Michelle heaved the grille out of the way.

I nodded. "Always be prepared. Okay, lower me down."

Four sets of hands began to feed me through the new hole in the playground. It was narrow and seemed to get narrower the farther I dropped into it. By the time my feet were on the floor, I was already pressed up against the door.

I looked at the lock. It was an old-fashioned five-lever mortise lock. I had just the thing. There was just one problem.

I couldn't reach it.

No matter how I squirmed, I couldn't get my hand to the pouch hanging on the back of my utility belt. I wasn't exactly stuck, but every time I tried to reach behind me, my elbow had an argument with the narrow walls. And every time, the walls won.

"Your youth." Piggot's manic voice floated through the vent again. *"My brains. Our ambition. Just think about it!"*

"I don't want to think about it!" Hari squealed. *"I wish I'd never even heard of you. You're crazy!"*

"What are you doing?" Julie was leaning into the hole. "We don't have long."

"I can't move," I explained. "It's too narrow."

"Let me down there, then. I'm smaller than you."

"But you don't know how to pick a lock."

"You're nervous. I understand, Hari," Piggot soothed. *"But there's nothing to worry about. Just imagine: immortality."*

"Well, it looks like I'm going to have to learn real fast. Come on!"

Four sets of hands lifted me out again.

"Okay," I said as I handed over my tools to Julie. "This is

the bolt retractor. This is the lever lifter. With this one you're lifting a lever that is holding the bolt locked. This one twists and pushes the bolt back. Got it?"

"Lift the lever, retract the bolt. Simple," Julie said. She nodded as I mimed the actions again.

"And Julie?"

"Yeah?"

"I know it doesn't feel like the right occasion for it, but don't rush. If you . . ."

"Nearly there," Piggot's voice interrupted again, as manic as ever. *"This tube goes in here, this tube goes in here, I press this, and then we sit tight."*

"Heeeelp!"

"Are you sure about that?" Julie wanted to know.

"Seriously!" I grabbed her shoulders. "If you lose the picture of the lock in your head, you could be at it for hours."

"Sure," said Julie with a nod. "Let's go."

When Julie was on the ground, I leaned in as far as I dared. I focused my headlamp on the lock and kept talking in the calmest voice I could manage.

"Angle it up. Good. Find the tension. Don't rush. If it feels wrong, try again. No big deal."

"I don't want to work for you anymore! Let me go!" Hari pleaded, his voice frail and high.

"What's a little pain when you have the rest of a long life to forget it?" Piggot's voice sounded woozy, almost as if he were drunk. *"Maybe we can sing something together. Take your mind off it?"*

Hari whimpered something unintelligible. Then I heard a wonderful sound.

Click.

"Got it!" Julie yelled.

"Who's that?" Hari yelled, coming back to life. *"I'm in here! Help!"*

"Relax, Hari," Piggot's voice was wavering more and more. *"Everything's going to be all right. All right . . . all right . . ."*

"It's okay, Hari! We're coming!" Julie grabbed the handle and pushed at the door. It gave an inch but no farther.

"You're going to have to kick it or something," Sally explained. "It's probably got a cupboard or shelves in front of it."

"Shelves!" Julie yelled five seconds later as her second kick did the trick. I made a mental note to ask her later how the heck she generated so much power in so little space. Right then didn't seem the appropriate time.

"Okay, put me down again!" I told the others.

With the door half open, I helped Julie kick and barge the rest of her way into Piggot's lab. When we'd finished, there was dust, glass, and splinters everywhere.

As the debris settled, two hospital-type beds came into focus. So did the figures on them: Hari and Piggot. Hari was strapped down to his bed; a pale and weakened Piggot was writhing on the one next to him.

"Soon. Soon," Piggot muttered. His eyeballs rolled back in his head.

"Help me!" Hari begged.

"This tube!" Julie drew my attention away to one long winding tube among many. One end snaked to Piggot's forearm, the other to Hari's. I tried not to look at the needles. "What's that?" Julie pointed to a dark fluid. It was making its way slowly from Piggot's end of the tube to Hari's.

"Well," I said, pinching the tube between Hari and the leading edge of the dark fluid. "I don't know the technical term for it, but for our purposes, I bet we can call it Piggot sauce."

"What are you doing?" Hari wailed, looking at my fingers on the tube.

"Just what I wanted to know," Julie seconded. "Don't worry about pinching it. Just get it out of his arm!"

"I don't like needles," I explained, keeping my grip. "And here are some other things I don't like, Hari: rival newspapers, people who suck up to authority, and, most of all, anyone who threatens to reveal my secret identity!"

"I won't, I promise!" Hari pleaded. "Just get me out of here."

"But how can I trust you?" I demanded, my fingers still gripping the tube.

"Because sometimes you just have to!" Julie answered for him. "Like me. Trusting me."

"And me," Sally agreed, making her entrance.

"Yep. Me too," Norris chipped in, dusting himself off. "We're on your side, remember. Just take the tube out."

I looked at my team. I looked down at the terrified face of my bitter rival.

For some reason, it didn't feel as good as it should have.

I grimaced and pulled the needle out of Hari's arm.

Julie came over to me with an empty bottle. "In here," she said. She put Hari's end of the tube into it. "And this time, it doesn't get locked in a cupboard. Agreed?"

I released my grip on the tube. The fluid made its way into the bottle. "Agreed."

We watched the last of Piggot's essence drain into the small bottle.

"Thanks," Hari said as we undid the straps on his wrists. "I mean it. I was wrong."

"Bit of an understatement," I suggested, but a groan from the other bed prevented me from going into further detail.

"Are you all right, Mr. Chattersly?" Sally was bent over the principal. He was looking pale and confused. "It's okay. Piggot is gone! Back in his bottle. The one that's just being stamped on by those boys."

Mr. Chattersly blinked and looked around. "But where am I? Where's he gone? What . . . happened?"

"Don't worry." Norris smiled and patted Hari on the back. "Hari's going to explain it to you. Every last word."

"Hari?" Chattersly pushed the name around feebly. He looked like a baby trying to remember what a spoon did again. I reached for my camera, but Julie made me put it back in my pocket.

"Who's Hari?" Chattersly wanted to know, his memory still struggling. "And who are you? What's your name?" he muttered, turning to face me. His eyes were still rapidly going in and out of focus.

"Oh, don't worry about that, Mr. Chattersly," I said cheerfully as we all headed back out to Michelle, who was offering us a hand up. "It's really not important."

TOP SECRET

Author Malcolm Judge lives in a large Cumbrian village in England with his wife and three sons. When he's not teaching drama, he enjoys cycling and refereeing at the local rugby club. Besides writing, he still likes the idea of becoming an international film star when he grows up.

EXCLUSIVE INTERVIEW
MALCOLM JUDGE

What was your favorite book as a kid?
The Hobbit by J.R.R. Tolkien. I've always
loved adventure stories and the success of the
underdog. As a young adult, my favorite book
was *Catch-22* by Joseph Heller. It was mad, bad,
and I couldn't put it down.

What is your favorite book now?
The Adventures of Huckleberry Finn by Mark
Twain. I just loved the incredible voice of Huck
and the whole romance of the epic raft journey.

How did you start writing?
I always loved writing at school. My school
did a mini-newspaper that went in the local
newspaper. It was called *The Willowbank Warbler*
and I did some sports reports. My first taste of
success was getting picked for the final fifteen of
a national writing competition.

What's your typical writing day?
I usually write twice a week for two to three hours each time.

What inspired you to write your book?
Jonny Jakes began life as a space pirate! I think the idea was simply to put two things together that I knew my sons would find interesting and see what happened.

What other jobs have you done?
Quite a few! Waiter, tree surgeon, and care worker to name three. I am currently a teacher, but when I grow up, I want to be an international film star.

What do you hope readers will think when they read your book?
I hope they laugh — a lot — but I also hope it will inspire the rebel in them and get them thinking about how to make a difference in their own world.

TOP SECRET

Illustrator Alan Brown's career as a freelance artist and designer has allowed him to work on a wide range of projects, from magazine illustration and game design to children's books. He's had the good fortune to work on comics such as Ben 10 and Bravest Warriors. Alan lives in Newcastle, England, with his wife, sons, and dog.

EXCLUSIVE INTERVIEW

ALAN BROWN

Who's your favorite character to draw?
Without a doubt, Mr. Jones from *Jonny Jakes Investigates the Hamburgers of Doom.*

Who's your favorite character overall?
Jonny — nothing stops him from getting to the truth.

What was your favorite book as a child?
My favorite books were *The Twits* by Roald Dahl, and a huge book on English folklore and myths my parents had. That's still my favorite book — it's really interesting to see where our traditions and beliefs come from.

How did you start illustrating?
I first got into illustration through doing storyboards for an ad agency. After many years working in graphic design, I've finally come back to my love of drawing. I've enjoyed working

on a great many jobs over the past few years, but the highlights are definitely drawing the *Ben 10 Omniverse* comics and, of course, working on *Jonny Jakes.*

Do you sketch by hand or digitally?
It all depends on deadlines. If it's a tight timescale, I work completely digital. But if I have the time, I prefer to draw traditionally, then work up the sketch digitally to create the final piece.

If you weren't an illustrator, what would you be and why?
Other than working as an illustrator, I've been a graphic designer and tattoo artist. But as a child, I always wanted to be one of the guys who works in the lab for James Bond, making rocket pens and invisible shoes.

What's your typical working day?
I usually get up at 4:30 a.m., grab a coffee, and start work. At 6:30 a.m., I walk the dog and make breakfast, then generally go back to work at 9 a.m. and work through until about 6 or 7 p.m. Long days, but I get paid to draw aliens . . . can't complain!

OUR TOP FOUR
FEATURED TEACHERS

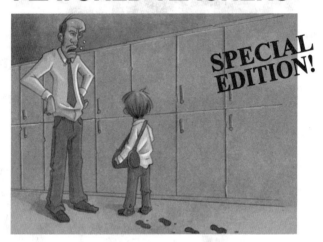

SPECIAL EDITION!

MR. HARDY

Despite his recent retirement, Mr. Hardy still tops our list. If it was wrong, he did it. If it was stupid, he said it.

Among the many columns dedicated to him, who can forget his wise words when asked to explain his policy on cell phones in school:

"The whole point of cell phones is to keep them safely in your lockers. Even better, keep them at home where they belong."

OUR TOP FOUR FEATURED TEACHERS

SPECIAL EDITION!

MR. JONES

He wasn't here for long, but Mr. Jones comes in a close second. He may have had more brains than the rest of the teachers put together, but that still wasn't enough to stop *TWW* from putting an end to his evil plans.

In an article wondering why he was always offering everybody candy, *TWW* once described him as "an intergalactic, purple-pigmented menace."

And that was before we realized what he was really up to.

OUR TOP FOUR
FEATURED TEACHERS

SPECIAL EDITION!

MR. CHATTERSLY

Mr. Chattersly quickly found himself on the front page. It took him only three days as Acting Principal to enact the controversial ban on novelty pencil toppers on the grounds of "health and safety." Even when he wasn't being possessed by the spirit of Victory Piggot, he still had a habit of attracting negative publicity.

When not at work, rumor has it that he likes nothing better than relaxing at home surrounded by his large collection of self-portraits.

OUR TOP FOUR
FEATURED TEACHERS

SPECIAL EDITION!

MS. BRIARS

Ms. Briars may be the worst teacher in the world, but that doesn't mean she isn't up for saving it every now and again. She lives in the drama studio, but when she is let out into the open, everyone knows about it.

After last semester, Ms. Briars became very famous on the internet. Unfortunately, she still can't make it work, so she has no idea how popular she is.

JONNY JAKES

Investigates

THE HAMBURGERS OF DOOM

When a new principal arrives halfway through the semester, Jonny smells a rat. Teachers handing out candy? All-you-can-eat hamburgers?

He's determined to get to the bottom of it, because Jonny Jakes investigates the same way he eats his hamburgers: with relish.

definitely NOT human

OUT NOW!